JENNIFER S. ALDERSON

A Killer Inheritance

First published by Traveling Life Press 2024

Copyright © 2024 by Jennifer S. Alderson

All rights reserved. No part of this publication may be reproduced, stored or transmitted in any form or by any means, electronic, mechanical, photocopying, recording, scanning, or otherwise without written permission from the publisher. It is illegal to copy this book, post it to a website, or distribute it by any other means without permission.

This novel is entirely a work of fiction. The names, characters and incidents portrayed in it are the work of the author's imagination. Any resemblance to actual persons, living or dead, events or localities is entirely coincidental.

First edition

ISBN: 9789083169774

This book was professionally typeset on Reedsy. Find out more at reedsy.com

Contents

1	Trapping A Fox	1
2	Dave Gets It Wrong	8
3	Awkward Moments	13
4	Antiques Time	19
5	Lights Out	33
6	Death On Set	39
7	Investigation Time	45
8	Questioning Cindy	51
9	Translating The Letters	54
10	Getting To Know The Crew	58
11	Interviewing Carmen	63
12	Stealing The Box	66
13	Bad Seeds	69
14	Checking In With Rhonda	73
15	Julie Shares A Secret	76
16	Wartime Grannies	81
17	Solving Another Puzzle	86
18	Another Break-In	90
19	Updates From Cindy	95
20	Charm Bracelet	100
21	Talking Through The Suspects List	103
22	Old Wounds	109
23	Tracking Down A Lead	115
24	Shaking Their Tail	120
25	Message Inscribed In Stone	125
26	Upsetting The Detective	128

27	In Search Of A Windmill	130
28	Going Underground	139
29	Treasure Found	144
30	Confession Time	148
31	Unexpected Savior	153
32	Bloody Fingerprint	157
33	Tiaras and Titles	159
34	Poorly Timed Ping	165
35	A Killer Inheritance	167
Acknowledgements		174
About the Author		175
Death on the Danube: A New Year's Murder in Budapest		177
The Lover's Portrait: An Art Mystery		180

1

Trapping A Fox

Dave Swanson twirled me around the dance floor like a pro. I hadn't cha-cha'ed in years, but in Dave's arms, it was a breeze to follow his lead. Especially since any missteps were easy to justify because my cover dictated that I appear to be extremely inebriated.

The ballroom was a gorgeous rectangular space, decorated to the nines in celebration of Princess Alexandria's sixty-third birthday. Hanging from the many chandeliers were streamers in gold and silver. Ice sculptures and champagne towers were placed strategically so that they were reflected in the antique mirrors covering the walls.

Placed upon one long table were the presents, now freed from their wrappings, that guests had brought for the princess. A few antique silver boxes, several pieces of jewelry, a small painting, many glass vases, and a multitude of other extravagant items were spread out for all to see, proof that she had rich friends with impeccable taste. Yet, as I took a closer look at the moldy stains on the ballroom ceiling and the wallpaper's curling corners, I did wonder whether the princess should consider selling her gifts off and using the profits to repair her castle, instead of using them to decorate her vast home.

Dave spun me around again, moving us away from the presents, just as the music built up to a crescendo before ending abruptly, the last notes hanging in the air. The small crowd applauded as the quartet stood to bow.

When Dave pulled me to his chest, I snuggled with him, inappropriately close for such a fancy occasion, and put my mouth next to his ear, as if I was whispering sweet nothings into it.

"Is Susan still watching me?" I asked, smiling widely.

"Yes," he replied so softly I barely heard him. Seconds later, he blushed and twitched his head, as if I'd said something highly unsuitable. He pulled back and raised an eyebrow at me. "I think you've had a few too many mai tais, my dear."

His boisterous tone ensured that everyone near us heard him. I just hoped my target did, too. "Mai tais" was my signal to let my knees buckle, sending me to the floor. The skirt of my emerald ballgown billowed out around me. I covered my mouth and gazed up at him with wide eyes, as if I was about to be sick.

"Oh, darling, what are we going to do with you? Let me help you up." Dave pulled me up by my armpits until I was vertical again, then grabbed my elbow and steered me towards the restroom just down the hall from the ballroom. I did my best to let my legs go all rubbery as I tripped and swayed my way across the dance floor, laughing my excuses to the other partygoers as I went.

After we reached the door to the ladies' room, I made a show of falling to the ground when he released his grip, and then giggling as I used the wall to slowly pull myself back up onto my towering heels. Over Dave's shoulder I spotted Princess Alexandria's assistant, Susan, already rushing to my assistance. When she took ahold of my arm to steady me, I had trouble hiding my smile. My little act had worked, after all.

"Can I assist you, ma'am?"

Dave answered for me. "Would you? She's had too much to drink, I'm afraid."

Susan steered me into the bathroom. "Do you feel sick?"

"Not exactly," I stammered as I pulled free from her grip, stumbled over to the nearest sink, and cranked open the tap. "I think I just need to splash some water on my face. The colder the better. The Baron is right; those mai tais are stronger than I'm used to."

"Of course, ma'am." Susan's tone and expression remained neutral as she stood back and watched. Considering how freely the alcohol was flowing at this party, I could assume Susan was used to dealing with her boss's drunken guests.

When I bent further over the sink, my diamond and emerald necklace—a vintage Cartier worth about three million dollars—swung forward. I let out a yelp and shifted uncomfortably, as if I was in pain.

I twisted and turned, as if I was trying in vain to loosen my jewelry from my clothing, but couldn't reach it, before locking eyes with Susan in the mirror. "Shoot, my necklace is stuck on my dress again. Would you mind untangling it?"

"Certainly."

I held the long wisps of my curly brown hair that had escaped from my updo away from my neck so she could get a better look at the clasp, then turned to face the mirror. For my plan to work, I needed her to see my eyes fluttering closed.

I could feel her pulling on the safety chain, a thin chain attached to either side of the expensive necklace that acted as a backup for the clasp. "The chain is caught up in the sequins. I need to get it loose, otherwise it's going to rip them off of your dress."

"I was afraid of that," I slurred. "Could you loosen the chain? It's been catching on the neckline all night. The clasp should be strong enough."

"Certainly, madam."

It was Dave's idea to let her get a good look at the clasp and have her remove the chain that ensured the expensive piece would not fall off of my neck.

I still did not believe Dave's theory that Princess Alexandria, Susan's employer, was a criminal mastermind known as the Silver Fox, but I had promised to help him out, regardless. It was the least I could do after walking out on the last of several unsuccessful dates.

I'd heard mention of the Silver Fox several times since Lady Sophie Rutherford, my official partner at the Rosewood Agency, and I had set foot in Europe two months earlier. At pretty much every party we had attended, there were victims of this thieving organization present, and they gladly shared their encounters with the rest. According to most of the Baroness's friends, it was the code name of a master thief who had been stealing gem-filled jewelry from the filthy rich for a number of years.

Yet whenever law enforcement agencies got a solid lead to one suspect, clues appeared that pointed to another. It was a never-ending circle of red herrings that the good guys couldn't seem to break through. At least, until now.

Several loose bits of new intel seemed to point to Princess Alexandria as being the spinner of the web. Which was why Dave had asked me to help him figure out whether that was the truth.

So here I was, dressed to the nines, as the date of the fictitious Baron von Trapp—or Dave Swanson of Interpol, preparing to set a trap that he hoped would result in the arrest of the princess. Honestly, when Dave had told me his true reasons for wanting to attend, I had made him repeat them because his accusations seemed too ridiculous. How could that dainty princess be the leader of an international criminal organization? But Interpol's intel didn't lie. Which was why he'd decided to set a trap at the next event on her social calendar, which was unfortunately her birthday party.

Given the time constraints, Dave decided the quickest way to test his theory would be for us to both be rowdy and boisterous. Me pretending to be too drunk to notice someone stealing my necklace was all part of the ruse. The tracker Dave's team had placed inside the gorgeous silver art deco piece would allow him to finally catch his target in the act of thievery.

Chances were high that not the princess, but one of her employees, would be doing the actual stealing—at their employer's bidding, of course. Which was why we spent the first hour watching the staff, looking for anything unusual. After Dave had spotted Susan lifting a diamond bracelet from one of the princess's aunts with the ease of a professional pickpocket, we'd decided to make her our target.

When Susan pulled on the chain rather sharply, catching several loose hairs as she did, I yelped. "Ouch. How are you doing back there?" I let my lower lip pucker out, but kept my eyes shut.

"I've almost got it. Could you lean over a little bit more? You're much taller than I."

I had to applaud her cunning mind. So I did as asked and stretched my neck farther over the sink, swaying forward as I did. It was crucial that Susan believed I was too intoxicated to really notice what was going on around me. She fumbled with the clasp, her thick fingers seemingly unable to loosen the safety chain. For effect, I breathed in heavily, as if I had momentarily drifted off and let my head fall forward even more, when Susan struck. If I hadn't been expecting it—or had truly been inebriated—I never would have noticed her loosening the clasp. Because the necklace was already hanging in the air, I hardly noticed it sliding off of my neck or falling into her waiting hand.

Once I was certain she'd pocketed her prize, I stumbled a little, banging my hip against the sink, before letting my eyes pop open and the many wisps of hair fall loose, covering my neck again. Susan was still watching me, her face as neutral as it was when she entered. I blinked slowly and wobbled a little on my feet as I rolled my neck. "Thanks, that's better. I just need to use the ladies'. I can see my way back to the dance floor."

"Certainly." She bowed ever so slightly before exiting. I barely noticed her slipping my necklace into her pocket as she turned towards the door. Her professionalism surprised me a little, but did help to confirm Dave's theory.

As soon as the bathroom door closed, I pulled out my phone and opened the tracking app so I could watch the necklace moving through the residence.

The tracker only worked at short range but was accurate to within twenty feet, which was perfect for our purposes. Dave assumed that somewhere hidden in Princess Alexandria's home was a stash of jewelry worth millions. With a little luck, our necklace would soon be added to the pile.

Susan and the necklace were still on the move, traveling farther into the spacious mansion the princess called home. I counted to a hundred before following our lead. When I opened the bathroom door slowly, I didn't see Dave waiting for me. Figuring he was already hot on the trail, I shot around the corner and into a wide hallway, decorated with a dark blue wallpaper and several seascapes, letting the blinking blip on my screen guide me.

Moments later, when the tracker stopped moving, I picked up my pace, following a maze of corridors until I reached a closed door at the end of a short hallway. Through the glass-paned door, I could see old hardbacks lining the walls.

"Of course," I sighed in frustration. A library offered many a hiding place, especially for those who knew it intimately. Not only could she have placed the necklace behind a stack of books, but she also may have hollowed out several old editions and placed the jewelry inside of them. Normally, searching through such a space could take hours, as I knew from previous experience. Yet with Dave's tracker, I was feeling pretty confident about being able to zero in on the target in a matter of minutes.

I laid my hand on the handle, my senses on high alert. I hadn't passed Susan, so I had to assume she had either taken a different route back to the ballroom or was still inside.

Ever so slowly, I pushed the door open and listened, but didn't hear anyone, so I slipped inside. As soon as I pulled the door shut behind me, I looked to my phone to orient myself. Just as my head dipped, Dave's popped out from behind a reading table. "Boo!"

I grabbed my chest and fell backwards. "Geez, Dave, you almost gave me a heart attack!"

"Sorry, but I couldn't help myself." He chuckled as he walked over to the bookcase in the far corner, where books had already been removed from several shelves. "The signal is coming from behind this wall. So either it's messed up, or there is a hidden room or space hidden behind this bookcase."

I bit my lip, wondering how deep it could be. "Do you know what's next door?"

"The outside wall. Can you help me look for a way in?"

I joined Dave in clearing the shelves, hoping to find a book that acted as a trigger, or a button or lever that would open a hidden space.

We'd just cleared the third shelf, when the library door opened and Susan rushed in. Dang, she must have noticed that I hadn't returned to the ballroom after the bathroom incident.

"What is the meaning of this? This library is private, and those books are expensive rare first editions. How dare you handle them so carelessly. The princess will be livid!"

I turned on my heel. "You know what else is going to upset her—hearing that you stole my necklace! Unless, of course, you did it for her."

Susan's hand flew to her chest. "Whatever do you mean? I tried to help you, remember? Or are you too drunk to recall? And how dare you accuse me or the princess of being involved in anything illicit!"

I straightened up. "For your information, I was pretending to be drunk so that you would think I would not be able to recall what happened to the necklace. But I saw you remove it and pocket it."

Susan was as cool as ice. "No, it was still around your neck when I left you to use the toilet. It must have fallen off afterwards. You had me remove the safety chain because it kept getting caught on your dress, remember?"

"You're lying. Want to know how I know?" I held up my phone, the screen lit up by the tracking app.

"You put a tracking device in the necklace?" Susan wavered on her feet, and her face grew ashen.

"You bet I did."

Before she could say another word, Dave pulled another first edition out of the bookshelf, and a section of the bookcase popped open. "What do we have here?"

He pulled the panel open, revealing my necklace atop a mini-mountain of jewelry that I would have guessed to be worth several million dollars. The jewels in the rings, bracelets, brooches, tiaras, and necklaces sparkled under my phone's flashlight.

Dave emitted a low wolf whistle. "Bingo."

2

Dave Gets It Wrong

Dave rocked back on his heels. "Your boss must be pleased with this evening's take," he said, his tone smug.

Instead of answering, Susan jutted her chin out and folded her arms over her torso.

"You stole these for Princess Alexandria, didn't you? Does she give you a cut, or is thievery simply part of your job description?" Based on his tone, it was clear Dave was feeling pretty confident that he had his culprit.

Susan eyed him critically. "Who are you?"

Dave puffed up his chest even further. "I'm not really a baron; I work for Interpol. We've been tracking the Silver Fox for years. If you testify against Alexandria, I promise the judge will look favorably on your actions and reduce your sentence."

Susan glared at Dave for what felt like a lifetime, until her thin lips finally flapped open. "I want a lawyer."

"Fine by me." Dave grabbed Susan by the arm and began pulling her towards the door. Over his shoulder, he called out to me, "I've already requested backup and told them to detain the princess as soon as they arrive. A few of my colleagues should be waiting for us in the driveway by now."

I crossed over to one of the many windows and noted that three cop cars were parked close to the entrance. By the time we reached the ballroom, the music had stopped, and instead of laughter and chatter, all I heard were furtive whispers as the guests tried to discern what was going on. When Dave passed through the ballroom with Susan in a firm grip, the gasps were audible.

We'd almost made it to the front door when Princess Alexandria's shrieks reached my ears. "Unhand me, you barbarian! I demand to speak with your superior." An officer stood close, one hand on her upper arm in a firm grip.

Dave smiled in a predatory way as he turned towards the princess and stuck out his hand. "That would be me. Dave Swanson of Interpol, the fine arts division. Shall we talk in private?"

He smiled as he gestured towards a sitting room just off of the foyer. Alexandria dipped her head in acknowledgement and followed him and Susan into the small space.

I closed the doors behind us, to the obvious disappointment of the gossip-mongering guests already flocking closer.

Dave released Susan's elbow and pointed to a pair of wingback chairs. "Take a seat, ladies. We have much to discuss."

Instead of doing as he requested, the princess strode over to Dave and glared up at him. "The impertinence! How dare you talk to me in such a tone."

"Gosh, lady. Sorry, but I don't have a lot of respect for thieves."

"Are you accusing me of thievery? Have you lost your mind?"

Dave grinned and scratched at his cheek. "Not that I'm aware of, princess. Or should I say, Silver Fox?"

The princess looked at him blankly, as if she had no idea what he meant. Her assistant, Susan, however, whitened so quickly I was worried she was about to pass out.

However, Dave, being on the roll that he was, somehow missed the women's reactions and barreled on.

"Susan, you stole the jewelry at Princess Alexandria's behest, isn't that right?" Dave held up his phone, the screen filled with a snapshot of the pile of jewelry hidden away in her library.

The princess gasped and clutched at her heart. "I have no idea what those rings and necklaces are doing in there. Susan, what do you know about this?"

Her assistant kept her gaze pointed forward, refusing to make eye contact with either interrogator.

Dave leaned in close to the royal. "Admit it, Alexandria, you are the Silver Fox. You have your minions stealing jewelry for you, in order to pay for the repairs to your many homes."

The princess's head flew back as if Dave had slapped her. "Why, I would never—"

"Come now, I heard you complaining earlier about how much maintaining this monstrosity costs, and how as soon as one wing of your castle is renovated, you have to start refurbishing the other."

It was during a brief tour of the castle earlier this evening that Dave had become convinced that Interpol's search was over, and that the princess was the mastermind behind the Silver Fox thefts. Her Swiss abode, one of several majestic homes she had inherited along with her royal title, was a ruinous castle close to the Italian border. The rooms were all exquisitely decorated with period pieces and antique furnishings that must have cost a fortune. But the furniture and artwork were in sharp contrast to the building itself. "Faded glory" was the phrase that came to mind. As glorious as her old castle was, it needed some serious maintenance work. In fact the tour had ended abruptly, after an elderly noble tripped over a loose floor tile. Princess Alexandria had blushed red and muttered her excuses, before leading us back to the dance floor.

When the royal clammed up, Dave turned back to Susan. "You don't have to be scared of retribution from Alexandria or any of her cronies. Just admit it and I can take care of you—the princess is the mastermind behind the Silver Fox crime ring, isn't she?" Dave pulled back and pointed an accusing finger at Alexandria.

Yet the royal merely shook her head. "Of all the silly ideas. I haven't asked Susan to steal anything. If you're too obtuse to see the truth, then let me do your job for you."

Alexandria turned to her assistant. "Susan, is it true what this fool is saying—are you are this Silver Fox? Is that why you have been stealing jewelry from my friends?"

Dave looked at both women, confusion etched on his face, but said nothing.

When Susan remained silent, the princess shook her head in disappointment. "I gave you time off to visit your sick mother and a yearly Christmas bonus. I treated you like family, and this is how you repay me?"

Susan's cackle filled the room. "Like family—you don't even know my name!"

The princess looked up at her assistant in confusion. "What do you mean? You've always answered to Susan."

"I admit, I do look quite a bit like my predecessor, but I'm not her. She got fed up with you calling her Susan and quit a few months ago."

The princess looked over her assistant blankly. "But Susan is your name?"

"No, it's not! It was the name of your assistant who quit years ago. Your previous assistant's name was Layla, and I'm Joanie. I was told when I started that part of my job was answering to the name Susan because somehow you got it in your privileged little head that we're all named Susan. When I balked, saying that you'd never believe me, your head housekeeper warned me that you barely paid attention to the help and wouldn't even notice that I wasn't the same person."

Princess Alexandria swooned, and for a moment there, I thought she was going to faint for real. "That can't be…" Her voice trailed off, and she averted her gaze to the parquet floor.

Susan huffed in irritation. "She was right! You and your friends are all alike. You barely acknowledge us, until we do something to displease you, and then you sack us without another thought. We have no pension plans, and if you badmouth us to one of your cronies, then we end up unemployable. We're interchangeable to you, but your gossip and catty remarks can cost us our livelihoods. But not a single one of you cares, which is why we created our own safety net."

"You are the Silver Fox?" Dave finally asked Susan, his tone incredulous. He was clearly having trouble wrapping his head around this development, despite having heard the woman's confession. I could understand his confusion. For the past two weeks, he had operated under the impression that our royal host was the Silver Fox, not the woman's household staff.

When Susan turned to face Dave again, her expression was no longer passive, but defiant. "There is no one Silver Fox, but a network of disgruntled housekeepers, cooks, chauffeurs, footmen, and butlers who are tired of being used and tossed aside. It was active long before I was approached about joining. After working here for a few weeks, I didn't need much convincing. I'm one of their newer members, but the organization grows in number exponentially every year. We may be unseen by you and your cronies, but trust me—we are everywhere."

3

Awkward Moments

After Dave's colleagues had arrested Susan and taken her away, Lady Sophie was allowed inside the room to comfort her dear friend, Princess Alexandria.

"I told you it wasn't her," Sophie breathed as she limped past me, leaning heavily on her cane. Her foot was now in a walking cast, but she found it painful to be up and around for too long.

It was thanks to the Baroness that Dave and I had been able to attend, under the guise of being a couple, and lay this trap for the Silver Fox. Because Sophie was a close friend of the princess, she had vehemently refused to believe that Alexandria could be the mastermind behind such an organization. Yet our boss had made clear that we were to help Interpol with this operation.

Now that we knew the Princess was not the mastermind, I was glad that the trap we had laid did not involve Sophie in any way. I would have felt terrible if this operation had damaged her relationship with her good friend.

We closed the door on the wailing princess, with the Baroness's arms wrapped firmly around her.

I leaned against the door. "Wow. So the Silver Fox isn't one person, but a conglomerate of housekeepers, drivers, and cooks who were creating their own retirement plan. Go figure."

When Dave ran a hand through his hair, I noted his face was still ashen. "I didn't see that coming, either."

He looked to the ground before clearing his throat. "Thanks for your help.

Could I take you to dinner tomorrow, as a way of showing my gratitude?"

Now that it was no longer necessary to pretend to be a couple, his tone was careful, and he kept his distance physically. I felt the same. After our last awkward date, we'd both agreed to put our potential relationship in the freezer for now. As much as I enjoyed his company and how his touch sent an electric spark running through my skin, I couldn't stop comparing everything he did with Carlos, my late husband.

It didn't take Dave long to figure out that he couldn't compete with a dead man. During our last meal together, he had made quite clear that he wanted to see me again, if and when I was able to see him for who he was, and not how he measured up against Carlos.

Who could blame him? I wouldn't have wanted to be put in that situation, either. And as much as I realized rationally that what I was doing was wrong, I couldn't help myself. My current obsession with finding Carlos's killer, and the fact that I might finally have a genuine lead to his whereabouts, wasn't helping me to forget the past and focus on the future, either. Perhaps once I had found Antonio and settled the score, I would be able to move on. But seeing as I had been tracking the elusive mob boss for almost four years, I did wonder when that moment would come, and whether Dave would wait around long enough to find out if we did have something special.

We'd been in casual contact ever since, but our messages were far more superficial and less intimate than they had been a few weeks ago.

I studied my Jimmy Choos, avoiding his gaze. "Sorry, I'm going to have to pass. I'm heading to Amsterdam first thing in the morning so I can see Rhonda's taping of *Antiques Time*, and I need to get packed."

"But a girl's got to eat." His eyes were pleading for me to say yes.

I sucked in my breath, not wanting to have this conversation now. Instead of justifying my decision to eat a takeaway sandwich in my room instead of joining him for a proper meal, I decided to ignore his request. "After she's done with the third taping, I'm hoping to have a little girl time with Rhonda that's not work-related."

Dave snorted. "As far as she is concerned, it's been nothing but girl time since she got here. You still haven't told her what you really do for a living, have you?"

I jerked back. "Of course not! I signed a confidentiality agreement, so I'm not blabbing to anyone."

"But you didn't have any assignments for the past two weeks—what did you two do?"

"I barely saw her because she was busy with Julie and then her show. Which is why I hope to take her away for a long weekend, when the show's crew moves the set from Amsterdam to Paris later this week."

After the conclusion of my last assignment, Rhonda and I had originally planned on heading to the French Riviera to soak up the sun. But neither of us had anticipated that she would be reunited with her estranged daughter, or that Rhonda's producer Cindy would be so enthusiastic about filming several shows in Europe, preferably as soon as possible so as to not disrupt their normal television season.

Which meant our trip to France didn't happen. After Julie and Rhonda spent a week bonding, Cindy showed up and whisked Rhonda away, introducing her to a number of local antiques experts who could help them with the prep work and organization of an appraisal day.

I couldn't complain, seeing as I had originally invited Rhonda to Europe in order to help me with a job. How could I be upset that she was now working on her own show?

"And where are you off to next?" I asked, intentionally shifting the conversation away from my life.

My question caused his gaze to drop to the ground. "On to a new case with a new team. I can't say much about it, I'm afraid."

"Here we go again," I mumbled. It wasn't just Carlos that stood in our way. Interpol and the Rosewood Agency, our respective employers, were not used to sharing intel, but keeping it from each other. As long as we played for different teams, we could not be open about our work, without risking losing our jobs—or even a jail sentence.

Not being able to be open or honest with each other had quickly taken its toll. Which made sense. Intimacy was challenging when you had to keep a large part of your life a secret. With my late husband, that had never been an issue. We could tell each other everything because we had worked for the same agency.

If I came out of retirement completely and went back to working full time as a recovery agent for the Rosewood Agency, could Dave and I ever make it work? It seemed highly unlikely, even if I could get over my obsession with Antonio. If only I was a civilian without any knowledge of the true nature of his work, then he could have pulled the wool over my eyes—as I had done to my loved ones for decades.

But the truth was he couldn't tell me about his day job any more than I could tell him about mine. And now I had even more secrets to keep. Dottoressa Esmerelda Bianci, an elderly lady claiming to be my great-aunt, had dropped into my life a few weeks ago and told me a stunner of a fact, before disappearing. While Rhonda had been busy with Julie and Cindy, I had flown down to Italy to try to talk with her again, only to be refused entry to her hospital room.

By the time I had tracked Bianci down, the old lady's health had declined so much that she'd been checked into a private hospital. I had tried to see her, but not speaking fluent Italian was a pretty good indicator that I was not immediate family. Apparently, it wouldn't have mattered because she had suffered a stroke and was almost incapable of communicating.

So now I was doing the next best thing—though a morbid one—and waiting for her to die. If she couldn't tell me the truth about my father, then hopefully one of her relatives could and would. All I could do now was wait for one of my Google alerts to go off, notifying me of her passing and the upcoming funeral.

Dave leaned over and pecked my cheek. It didn't have the same electricity as before, but it didn't feel wrong either. Instead of thinking of what could have been, I excused myself and sought my partner, still comforting Princess Alexandria in the salon.

It was clear from her wails that it was going to take the royal quite some time to accept her staff members' betrayal.

"Lady Sophie, may I speak with you?"

My partner untangled herself from her friend. Princess Alexandria wiped at her tear-stained face before rising. "I should tidy up my appearance."

After the princess had excused herself, my partner turned to me, defiance etched on her face. "I told you Alexandria wasn't the Silver Fox."

I bowed my head in humble resignation. "That may be, but even you have to agree that Interpol's evidence was strong. Besides, it was worth pursuing, and we did roll up at least part of the network."

When she jutted her chin out, I cocked my head at her, not wanting to play this silly game. "Now that we have this case wrapped up, I'm going back to Amsterdam to see Rhonda's show and meet up with Myrtle. Do you want to join me or would you rather stay here a while longer?"

"I'd rather stay. Alexandria needs a trusted friend right now. Besides, there is no rush to move on, is there? As far as I am aware, we've completed all of our assignments."

"You're right, we have nothing on our agenda, and I can imagine she appreciates your support right now." Honestly, I didn't care one way or the other if Sophie came back to Amsterdam with me. Maybe it was for the best, I realized, especially since she and Rhonda had butted heads during our last assignment. All that was important to me right now was seeing my friend tape her second show, live in person.

I had been a little miffed that I hadn't been able to attend the first taping because of this gig, but at least Rhonda's producer had set up a live stream for me to watch from my hotel room earlier this afternoon, before I helped Dave unmask the Silver Fox.

Yet I knew I couldn't complain about the work or ask Reggie to find a replacement. From what Myrtle had told me during our last conversation, it sounded like the Baroness and I were out of work. The next and last party on our assignment list had been canceled due to the target's unexpected death by heart attack. Another object I was hoping to search for, if I ending up having some spare time, had already been verified—albeit accidentally—by another agent who happened to be invited to a private party at the target's home. The Jean Miro painting we suspected she possessed was not the original, but a well-made copy signed by none other than Cyril Bouve. That discovery had made me chuckle. How small was the world?

With no assignments looming on the horizon, it appeared that our European adventure had come to an end. Part of me hoped Reggie would find us another assignment before we flew back to the States. Although, since the Baroness's foot was still in a cast, I suspected he'd wait to reassign us, until her leg had fully healed.

The Baroness smiled up at me faintly. "I'm certain Reggie can find us another assignment—if you want to keep working for the Rosewood Agency, that is."

"I think I do, but I have a few other things I'd like to do first." Her perceptive reply made me chuckle. We had gotten to know each other quite well during the past decade.

"Such as?"

Where to start, I thought. I had kept so much from her—and from everyone I loved—for so long. Now wasn't the moment to change things up. "Rhonda and I are still talking about visiting the French Riviera."

"That does sound lovely, especially this time of year." Sophie hesitated long enough to pick an invisible piece of lint off of her dress. "So it has nothing to do with that thing in Italy you refuse to tell me about?"

I shook my head. "No, it doesn't. And I will tell you everything, once I get it all sorted out in my mind." I wasn't ready to tell her about the funeral I expected to happen, or my search for my husband's killer. I hoped to do so, once I had something concrete to share.

But for now, the rest could wait. I had a taping to attend, one I wouldn't miss for the world.

4

Antiques Time

I blinked furiously as the plethora of bright lamps hanging from a spiderweb of black scaffolding flickered on, exposing the complexity of the impromptu stage built before us. The glorious New Church in Amsterdam was the perfect backdrop for a taping of my best friend's show—*Antiques Time with Rhonda Rhodes.*

The church was a fantastic find, on Cindy's part. The massive building was lit up by new and old stained-glass windows. The contemporary and ancient religious scenes, in combination with the richly colored glass, made my heart sing. The "ship" of the church, or nave, was a wide space with carved wooden pews on either side of a marble-tiled aisle that provided plenty of room for both the set and audience. A small oval-shaped stage had been built directly under a massive pipe organ that covered most of the wall, a gorgeous instrument that had been painted with scenes from the Bible. According to the accompanying sign, it was the largest pipe organ in the Netherlands.

A trio of cameras had been placed in front of the stage, aimed towards the pair of chairs already on it, presumably to be used by the show's host and guest. Just out of the camera's view were two long tables upon which the items to be featured on the show had already been laid out.

About a third of the audience members were actually participants in the show, here to have their items appraised live on the air. The rest had taken advantage of the free tickets offered to those interested in being a member of the live studio audience. Rhonda had mentioned that there was room for a hundred people, and when I looked back from my seat in the first row, I couldn't see any empty chairs.

From the positions of the other cameras placed strategically around the space, I was certain the director would have a gorgeous religious statue or stained-glass window in every shot. The lighting was quite dramatic, leaving most of the stage in darkness with three spotlights beaming down on the small table and the pair of chairs. Behind each camera stood an operator, yet the podium was still empty. It looked as if everyone was ready and all we were doing now was waiting for our host to arrive so the taping could begin.

I examined the antiques that Rhonda would be appraising today. The objects ranged from silver candlesticks to sketches by famous Dutch artists and even a stained-glass room divider. Based on my chats with several of the owners, I suspected they were all convinced they had brought in an object of great value. Most, however, would be wrong. I had already examined what was on offer, and much of it was not worth more than a few grand. But I knew from Rhonda's previous shows that beauty was in the eye of the beholder, and often the owner's stories about their beloved antiques were worth their weight in television gold.

I glanced behind the filled pews, towards the gray curtain running along the two sides and back of the church's ship, effectively creating an intimate studio space within the massive church. A slit on the left-hand side opened up onto a narrow passage way that led to the restrooms, a makeshift dressing room, and the director's booth.

I took in the public seated behind me. Based on the visible wrinkles, plastic surgery scars, and conservative clothing styles, I placed the average age of the audience members at sixty-five. Especially considering that the taping started at 10:00 a.m., most must have been retired already to have the free time to sit here for three hours.

Or perhaps they were just like Myrtle and I, employed but with a valid reason for wanting to be present. I looked over to my company contact, wondering whether this was the right moment to ask her about Mac's phone, even though I knew it was not. She'd arrived in Amsterdam while I was flying to Switzerland and had gotten to see the first taping yesterday. Which was good considering she'd flown over with the intention of meeting Rhonda in person. Both Myrtle and my boss, Reggie Rosewood, were huge fans of the show. Reggie had even hinted that he was considering asking Rhonda to work with his agency after she'd successfully helped me to recover a stolen statue a few weeks ago. However, Sophie or I were not enthusiastic about that possibility. As much as I loved Rhonda, discretion was not her forte, meaning she was not exactly a great candidate for the job.

I cast a sideways glance at my company contact, seated next to me and currently surfing the web on her phone. In contrast to my gown-wearing partner, Myrtle favored well-worn jeans and button-down shirts that looked to have been designed for a man's body. Despite having access to a richly filled bank account, she didn't spend much of it on personal styling, as far as I could tell. Her current haircut was a perfect example. It looked like Myrtle had skipped a trip to a salon and instead had taken a pair of sheep's shears to her head, because whoever did her buzz cut last, messed it up pretty badly. Not only was it uneven, bits of scalp were visible where they'd cut too close to her skin on the back of her neck.

I sat next to her in an uncomfortable silence, at a loss for something to talk about. Myrtle had been assigned to be my company contact on my first day as an art recovery specialist for the Rosewood Agency. Although we had worked together for fifteen years before I took an early retirement, she had always treated me as a junior rookie and never the senior sleuth I had become. It made our conversations about anything other than work challenging. So we sat in silence next to each other, waiting for the show to begin.

I looked around again, wondering from which side Rhonda would enter, when I suddenly felt a breath of warm air on my neck.

"How do I look?"

Some sleuth I was; I hadn't even noticed Rhonda's approach. I practically jumped out of my chair from the shock, but luckily my bestie didn't seem to notice. She was far too nervous about the taping. I turned to take in her relatively conservative ensemble—at least for Rhonda's tastes. Her ample torso was covered by the high neckline, which, given all of the closeups taken of the objects displayed on the desk, I had to assume was a deliberate choice. Otherwise the fabric was as bright and flowery as I was accustomed to seeing, and the cut of the dress helped to accentuate her curvaceous figure. Rhonda exercised regularly and was by no mean obese, but she was a voluptuous woman with a healthy appetite.

"Wow—you look amazing! Your makeup artist is a star. I mean, you always look good, but now you look like you're ready for the catwalk," I gushed, knowing that she was always nervous before taping started. But Rhonda always insisted it was healthy to be a bit nervous, that it kept her on her toes. And I knew from watching previous tapings that as soon as the director yelled out "action," she was as cool as a cucumber.

"I'm so proud of you!"

"Break a leg, Rhonda," Myrtle cheered, blushing as she did. We had arrived at nine to watch the setup, and Myrtle had been in full fangirl mode all morning. She couldn't seem to stop stuttering, until Rhonda had wrapped her up in a bear hug and erased any tension Myrtle had been feeling. The two had taken an immediate shine to each other, almost as if they had been great friends in previous life. It was wonderful to see, especially since Rhonda and my partner still seemed to be at odds.

Before Rhonda could respond to Myrtle, the show's producer rushed over with a microphone in her hand. I'd only met Cindy a few times, but knew that the tiny woman was a force to be reckoned with. "I need to switch out your mic, Rhonda. That one keeps cutting out."

Cindy didn't acknowledge Myrtle or me, but I knew not to take it personally. Instead, I tried to imagine how stressful it was for her to have to change out her star's microphone mere minutes before going live on social media.

Apparently, Rhonda felt the same tension. "No problem, Cindy. Say, you seem more stressed than normal. Is there anything I need to know about?"

Cindy unclipped the microphone from Rhonda's neckline and pulled out the long cord running across her back, grumbling the entire time. "Naw, it's just been one problem after another since we set up the studio in this church. I'm glad we have one show already in the can, but you better keep your fingers and toes crossed that everything works until we get the last two shows taped."

Once she'd switched the mic out for the new one, she stepped back and patted Rhonda's dress down. "You look fantastic, as usual. Do you need anything else or are we ready to roll?"

Rhonda's answering smile lit up the room. "As ready as I'll ever be. Let's get this one done and dusted, shall we?"

The two high-fived, before Cindy grabbed ahold of Rhonda's elbow and walked her up to the podium, whispering as she went. The crowd went wild as soon as she stepped up onto the stage, clapping and whistling loudly, as if she was a rock star. By the time Rhonda's butt hit the chair, her grin was so wide that I knew this was going to be a good show.

Cindy ducked behind the curtain, and for a second I saw the director, a Dutchman named Anton Berhard, huddled behind a bank of monitors set up to one side of the podium. He had been so agitated and snippy with everyone during this morning's preshow check that I had pulled my bestie aside to ask about him. She wasn't a fan of the director, which was rather unusual. Rhonda usually loved everyone.

Rhonda closed her eyes and breathed in deeply, clearly already relaxing under the spotlights. After she opened her eyes again, she pointed to the center camera and then gave it a thumbs-up. When the red lamp on top of camera one lit up, Rhonda was already beaming into the lens. "Well, howdy folks! Thanks for joining me today. We are once again filming from inside this glorious old church in the center of Amsterdam. Cindy, let's give our viewers at home another look at this marvelous building."

As the camera pulled out to a wide shot, Rhonda tittered into the microphone. "I should clarify, the official name of this glorious space is the New Church of Amsterdam. I tell you what, if this is the new one, I can't wait to see the Old Church!"

As I took in the colorful windows, organ, and the table of collectibles to be appraised, I couldn't help but be amazed that Cindy was able to set these three tapings up in just two weeks' time. Although Rhonda had initially expressed concern that the short timespan wouldn't allow for a sufficient number of items to be appraised, they'd been quickly overwhelmed with objects as soon as the ads for *Antiques Time* went live on the local cultural shows and magazines.

It turned out that there was a long-running and popular Dutch program called *Tussen Kunst en Kitsch* that had been doing something similar for years, so the locals had their antiques and collectibles ready to go—enough so that they quickly filled the three shows. I only hoped for Rhonda's sake that they would have similar luck for the upcoming shows in Prague and Paris.

The Dutch show's popularity also helped solve another problem that had concerned Rhonda. In the American version, she personally appraised all of the objects, live on-air. Yet her extensive knowledge was specifically geared towards the American market, and she and Cindy suspected that Rhonda might never have seen items similar to what would be brought in.

So instead of sticking to her normal routine, she had chosen to work with the local show's team of experts to appraise everything that had been brought in during the open days Cindy had organized.

With the help of their experts, Rhonda and Cindy had whittled the thousands of items down to sixty—twenty for each show. The plan was to invite each of the owners onto the stage for a chat about what the item meant to them, before she revealed the object's worth. That was where Rhonda excelled, helping to personalize the featured items so that the viewer was emotionally invested.

From the three hours that they taped each day, only about forty-five minutes of the most interesting footage would make the final cut. Because this was their first foray into international territories, Cindy had set up a special YouTube channel so that fans of the show could also watch the longer taping, live online.

When the first preselected guest walked over to the podium, followed by a crew member holding a Murano vase that I guessed to be worth two grand in her gloved hands, Rhonda looked across the crowd, all smiles.

Only once the guest was seated and the crew member out of the camera's shot did Rhonda tell the enthusiastic audience about the vase, its origins, and maker, eliciting many oohs and aahs from the owner and public as she spoke, before finally revealing its value. The glass and her story reminded me of our glorious visit to Venice and the glassmaking factories on the island of Murano a few weeks ago with Rhonda and her daughter Julie.

My bestie's delivery was so smooth and seemed so spontaneous—she really was a natural. After she'd finished to a standing ovation, the lady with the vase exited, and an even older woman took her place. Two members of the crew brought out a painting with a wide gilded frame and set it gently on an easel they'd set up next to Rhonda.

She quickly put the woman at ease before explaining why the Dutch artist's sketch was so important to his oeuvre, as well as the artistic movement he had been a part of, before revealing the sketch's current worth. Tears of joy sprung into the woman's eyes as she processed the substantial amount.

The second guest was quickly replaced with another. Several fascinating objects crossed the podium, a few of which I had not been able to place in context, at least not without having to search online for more information.

It was a joy to watch my friend at work. Rhonda shone, not only through her expertise, but also by the way she put her guests at ease. Yet after almost three hours of sitting still under the warm lights and listening to her chitchat, I could feel my eyelids sliding closed. I pinched my thumb to keep myself alert, knowing I could not nod off. Rhonda would never forgive me if I did.

Luckily for me, the last guest's object was fascinating enough to wake me back up.

When a scruffy young man named Jan Mank walked onto the podium, followed by a crew member holding a wooden box in her gloved hands, the crowd began to clap and cheer. The box was about the length and width of a shoebox and covered in an intricate pattern of inlaid wood. I hadn't seen anything so beautiful or well-crafted in quite a while.

I sat up straighter in my chair, straining to get a better look at it. It was the same Japanese puzzle box that Jan had brought onto yesterday's show. Rhonda hadn't been able to open it then, so she'd asked whether he'd leave it with her for the night and return to the show today, in the hopes she could figure it out.

I sure hoped Rhonda could get it open during this episode. Even since I'd seen it on-air, I couldn't stop wondering what was inside. I wasn't the only one curious to find out. The Dutch media had eaten the story up and featured it on the national news last night, which would account for why the church had filled up so quickly this morning. Speculation ranged from missing jewels to a treasure map, but until someone could get it open, all we could do was guess.

As pretty as the inlay work was, it was the story behind the box that made it so intriguing. His grandfather had left this box to his father, but Jan had only recently discovered it in a dusty old crate at his family home, soon after his father's passing. Uncertain of how to open it or what it may contain, Jan saw advertisements for Rhonda's upcoming show and brought it to her appraisal day, in the hopes of learning more about it.

Jan took a seat across from Rhonda, his face stricken as he did his best not to stare into the camera's lens. Whether it was the hunch of his back or the wideness of his doelike eyes, there was something about him that made me want to protect him. By the look on Rhonda's face, she was having the same reaction.

"Welcome back, Jan." Rhonda patted his hand lightly, in a failed attempt to put the young man at ease. He pulled at his collar as if it was too tight and stared at her with those big eyes.

She turned back to the camera, all smiles. "Well, viewers, what we have here is a Japanese puzzle box, and quite a fine one, at that. The inlaid pattern helps to hide the levers that open a secret compartment. But this isn't any old puzzle box. Yesterday's viewers may recognize this as being handcrafted by Jan's grandfather, a famous carpenter before the Second World War. Isn't that right, Jan?"

The young man giggled nervously when she mentioned his name. "Yes, ma'am. Granddad was well-known for his furniture and these puzzle boxes, thanks to the intricate inlay work that characterized his designs. I never got to meet him because he was killed a few days after WWII ended."

Rhonda's hand flew to her mouth. "That's horrible! What happened to him?"

"No one knows for certain. He and my grandmother were both found shot dead in their living room, and their house had been ransacked. Their murders have remained unsolved to this day. On the surface, their murders made no sense, unless their deaths had something to do with my granddad's work for the resistance."

It took me a minute to place his comment, until I recalled that he had shared quite a bit about his family history on yesterday's show. Because his father had never spoken of his granddad's past, he'd had to glean information about the old man from a few letters he'd found dispersed through the boxes and crates. Apparently the young man's granddad had been in the Dutch resistance and had helped several families move their most valuable possessions—primarily artwork—to bunkers located in the south of the Netherlands, for safekeeping.

Rhonda brushed a tear from her eye, her mouth pulling down at both corners. "That must have been hard on your father, growing up without his parents during such a volatile time in history."

He nodded. "He wasn't the only one orphaned by the war, but it definitely affected him. His parents had sent him to live with relatives outside of the city just before the war started, but they stayed in Amsterdam, I suppose to help with the resistance. When Dad came home after the war, he was the one who found his parents' bodies."

When Jan wiped a tear from his eyes, Rhonda did the same. "He suffered from bouts of depression most of his life and didn't let anyone get close, not even me or my mother. Finding his parents' bodies, along with the horrors of the war, made him who he was, I suspect."

Rhonda leaned in so close their knees were practically touching.

"But your dad didn't share anything else about his parents—your grandparents—with you?"

Jan shook his head. "Dad couldn't talk about his parents without crying, so I learned early not to ask about them. It didn't help that my mother died of pneumonia when I was young. And now that Dad is gone, I am well and truly alone..."

When his voice trailed off again, Rhonda sprung up and wrapped the young man up in a bear hug. I couldn't help but look away as she rocked him gently. I hoped for both of their sakes that Cindy would cut this from the final show, but then again, both she and Rhonda did tend to treasure the more emotional moments of the program. Apparently those tearjerkers were good for the ratings.

I looked away in embarrassment, to see Cindy's assistant, Theresa, rushing along one side of the curtain and towards the backstage, shooing a stagehand along as she did.

Before I could puzzle out what they were doing, Rhonda released Jan from her embrace.

The young man cleared his throat before reaching into his jacket pocket and pulling out several envelopes. "After we talked yesterday, I searched through Dad's belongings again and found a box of letters Granddad had written to him. After reading through them, I'm even more convinced that my granddad was an important member of a Dutch resistance group, and that he may have been killed by another member—one of several men that he referred to as 'bad seeds.'"

Rhonda's hands flew to the side of her face. "That's fascinating! Why do you think that?"

"In his last letter, Granddad wrote about a few profiteers that had infiltrated the group and stolen trucks filled with artwork that the Klavers resistance group meant to move down south. In April 1945, Granddad had stolen back a truck that the bad seeds had absconded with. From what he wrote, it sounds like he may have hidden the artwork away, but Granddad was quite vague about where. But he did mention this box and how Dad needed to keep it safe. If Granddad did hide the art away, this puzzle box may hold the key to finding it."

"Now that is exciting!" Rhonda exclaimed.

The young man leaned forward, nodding enthusiastically. "So, did you figure out how to open it?"

Rhonda giggled. "Lucky for you, I do have a few ideas of how we can get into it. But before we try, can you tell us why you are hoping there is something valuable inside?"

Jan blushed and averted his eyes. "I've been accepted into an American university, but the travel and tuition will be so expensive that I can't afford to go. Dad didn't leave me much in the way of an inheritance, so unless I can find something in Dad's things that's worth enough, I won't be able to."

While he was talking, Rhonda had donned gloves and lifted the box gently from the table. "I hope for you that whatever's inside is worth a fortune! Now, there should be a secret compartment in here somewhere. I spent the evening researching the most common solutions for these puzzle boxes and believe I know how to open this one."

"I'm keeping my fingers crossed," the young man said softly and blushed again. It was a good thing they had him mic'ed, otherwise no one would have understood his response.

What a sweet kid, I thought.

"Let's see if we can figure this out." Rhonda stared at the rectangular box for a moment before pushing in a few of the inlaid pieces. I held my breath, but nothing happened.

She then begun to feel around the sides and bottom, poking at the inlaid wooden strips as if they might pop open or depress. The longer she worked, the more the point of her tongue stuck out from between her lips. She kept fiddling with the panels, but it felt as if she wasn't going to succeed after all. Precisely at that moment, Rhonda used three fingers to push on three panels at the same time, and a soft click was audible.

I elbowed Myrtle. "Did you hear that?"

Jan's jaw fell open as Rhonda pushed another panel, and a tiny lid opened in the center of one side.

Rhonda turned to the young man and asked, "It looks like we should pull on that tab sticking out there. Would you do the honors?"

The young man nodded and did so, slowly releasing another panel. When Rhonda pushed on the newly exposed block, a spring must have triggered, because a hidden drawer popped out on the opposite side.

The audience—along with everyone watching, I suspected—gasped simultaneously. Rhonda beamed. "It looks like there's something inside."

He pulled the drawer open, and a lump of color seemed to spring up. The young man looked at it, puzzled.

"What is that?" I asked Myrtle.

She shook her head. "I do not know."

He lifted it up in the air, and the camera zoomed in. I squinted at the object in his hand. "Is that a woolen scarf?"

The young man let one end of the object go, and it unrolled automatically. Myrtle squinted at it. "It sure does look like a scarf, but a poorly knitted one."

When the camera zoomed in, I could see on the monitor that it was a tacky thing in shades of orange and red that seemed to have been made by an amateur knitter. The closeups made me think Myrtle was correct. It appeared to be unevenly knit and even lumpy in places. What a letdown. I'd been imagining all sorts of jewels and rare objects, but not this. I could only imagine how disappointed the grandson was.

"That's it—there's nothing else inside? What is the meaning of this?" Jan cried. He let the scarf fall to the ground and shoved his hand into the open drawer, but soon came back empty-handed.

Rhonda took his hand. "I don't understand it either. Your granddad went to a lot of trouble to hide this; you would have expected it to have more value. But it's just a common scarf, and not very well knitted, I'm afraid."

Jan pulled out of her grasp, his hands forming fists on his knees. "I was a fool to think this would pay for my college. Dad didn't leave me much, but the way Granddad wrote about this box's importance convinced me that he'd hidden something valuable inside. But a poorly knitted scarf isn't going to pay for four years at an American university."

When he began to weep, Rhonda patted his back. I could tell by the glint in her eye that she was about to go Oprah on him. "You've been through so much and have no one to take care of you anymore. Let me help you get to the United States. I'll sponsor your visa and pay your tuition fees."

I swore I heard someone cry out in anger, just before the crowd erupted in applause and Jan fell into Rhonda's arms. And rightfully so; in the States a college education these days cost far more than most middle-class American families, let alone desolate European orphans, could afford.

"Isn't she wonderful? You're so lucky to have a friend like Rhonda in your life, Carmen," Myrtle enthused as she wiped away a tear.

"You are right, she's amazing." I looked over the crowd, trying to work out who had cried out in what to me had sounded like anger.

But before I could, another commotion to the left of the stage caught my eye. Because I had been so focused on what was inside of the puzzle box, I hadn't noticed that the director had come out from behind the gray curtain and was whispering into one cameraman's ears. Whatever he said didn't seem to please the cameraman, and the large man's angry gestures were a bit distracting. Seconds later, both men began to fiddle with the cables.

Soon, Anton the director unplugged the cameraman's headphone and made a slicing gesture along his throat. The operator removed his headset and, with his shoulders rounded over in defeat, followed Anton back behind the curtain, leaving his camera unmanned.

From their actions and gestures, all I could think was that the equipment wasn't working properly. Poor Cindy, it had been one problem after another with this shoot. At least this taping was wrapping up, I thought. With a little luck, the third and final show to be taped in this church would run more smoothly.

I looked back up to the podium just as Jan pulled out of Rhonda's long embrace.

"Thanks for joining us here today, Jan. It was truly an honor to meet you and learn about your family. I can't wait to see how well you do with your studies."

The crowd's enthusiastic clapping drowned out his answer, but his smile was heartfelt and genuine.

When she turned back to the lens, the cameraman zoomed in on Rhonda. She grinned into the lens, yet remained silent. I thought there might be another glitch, until I realized she was waiting for Jan to leave the stage before wrapping up the show.

Only after the young man was out of the shot did a stagehand tap Jan on the shoulder, signaling that it was time to go. When Jan rose, he grabbed the scarf and puzzle box, before following the stagehand through the curtains and past the director's booth, presumably to the backstage dressing room.

After he had exited, Rhonda smiled broadly into the camera's lens and began closing down the show. "Well, folks, that's all we have time for today. I want to thank all my guests for sharing their treasures and cherished memories with us. It was a pleasure to get to know all of them better." When she gazed over the seated audience, seemingly making eye contact with all, I gazed up at my bestie, in awe of her ease with the camera and crowd.

At least, until a shrill cry rang out. From behind the curtain, I could hear Cindy yelling, "Where's that smoke coming from? Somebody get Rhonda out of there!"

5

Lights Out

Cindy's scream sent the audience members into full panic mode and crowding into the aisles leading to the main exit.

I looked over at my bestie, a few feet away on the podium, just as a surge of white light temporarily blinded me. A strange sizzling sound coursed through the space, accompanied by bursts of sparks emitting from the many electrical connections, before all of the electricity cut out. Before I could pinpoint the source of the smoke quickly filling the room, another crashing noise drew my attention to the darkened void that was the podium, where Rhonda was still sitting, moments before my bestie's screams filled the room.

"Rhonda—are you alright?" I screeched as I rose to go to her aid. Holding my hands out in front of me, I slowly moved towards Rhonda's voice. However, with my second step my leg caught the edge of a chair or cable, I couldn't be certain, tripping me up. "Drat—I can't see anything! Let me get my phone out."

"Take your time. I'm okay, I think. I must have cut my knee on something, that's all."

Just as I hit the flashlight button on my phone, the spotlights mounted into the church's ceiling flooded the room again.

Blinded by the sudden illumination, I tripped again. When I tried to steady myself, my fingers caught the sharp edge of something.

"Oh, no," I mumbled. That gorgeous screen made of stained glass was hanging off of the table, a large section of it broken. Shattered glass in a rainbow of colors covered the floor and podium. Rhonda was sitting on the edge of the stage, with one hand clamped over her leg, but the pressure wasn't enough to stop the trickle of blood from flowing down her calf.

"Be careful—there's broken glass on the podium, too," Rhonda warned.

I shuffled through the splinters of glass and rushed over to her. As much as I wanted to hug Rhonda, I didn't know how much glass was embedded in her clothes or skin. Considering I wanted to comfort her, not accidentally harm her further, I skipped it. "What happened?"

"When the lights went out, I panicked and sprung off the podium, but I must have smashed into that screen, when I did. I think there's some glass embedded in my knee now. I feel terrible that I broke one of the antiques brought in by an audience member, but luckily it wasn't worth much. Still, I do hope we're insured and the owner will accept my apology."

I shook my head. "Oh, hon, nobody could accuse you of negligence. Besides, I'm sure your show has insurance to cover such incidents."

"Rhonda—thank heavens you're alive!" Cindy cried as she tore out of the makeshift production booth and over the stage, towards the show's star. She grabbed Rhonda's arm and looked to the blood trickling out of her elbow, before studying her knee. "Let me get a good look at your face."

Cindy gently turned Rhonda's head left and right, carefully pulling a few shards out of her hair as she did. "The scratches aren't too deep, nothing a little makeup can't cover up," she murmured.

As soon as she'd completed her examination, Cindy pulled her star in for a hug. "Oh, Rhonda, you had me scared there."

Rhonda patted her hair. "There, there, everything's fine. I just lost my orientation and panicked when the lights went out. If I'd stayed in my chair, none of this would have happened."

Cindy pulled back, looking more satisfied than she did a moment ago. "I think you're going to be okay, but I still need a paramedic to examine you. I'm afraid they are going to have dig out that glass lodged in your knee."

Rhonda began to protest, but Cindy held up her hand. "Our insurance dictates it, otherwise we can't continue filming. That's why I've already called an ambulance."

Her words did the trick, and Rhonda's shoulders sagged in submission. "Okay, since you insist. But I still don't understand what happened. Do either of you?"

"Something must have short-circuited. Maybe one of the lights?" I suggested, as if I knew what I was talking about.

"One of the electrical boxes in the hallway began to smoke just before a power surge caused the electricity to cut out," Cindy answered in an authoritative voice. "Which in and of itself isn't strange; this church is quite old, and the show's gear is sucking up quite a bit of electricity."

She ran a hand through her spiky blond hair. "It's been one disaster after the other since we set up in here. It must be the graves that we're walking over. Their ghosts must not approve," Cindy said, then shivered and hugged her arms around her own body.

"Oh, Cindy, you don't really believe that this is the work of ghosts?" Rhonda whispered.

Buried under the floor were the mortal remains of the city's wealthiest and most notable citizens, at least those whose funerals had taken place before 1865 when the practice was stopped. According to the church's informational pamphlet, there were approximately ten thousand bodies lying under our feet in permanent rest. Even though I did not believe in ghosts, the sheer number, combined with the fact that the floor was in fact a series of grave slabs inscribed with the names of the dead, did feel slightly creepy.

"I don't know what to believe. But I do need to try to resolve this crisis in an earthly fashion. The health and safety people won't let us continue filming, until we do. Don't you worry; by the time we're ready to film again, we'll have everything sorted out."

Rhonda patted her producer's hand. "I know you will. I have faith in you."

Cindy began to walk back to the monitors, when she paused next to the table full of antiques. "Where's the puzzle box?"

"Jan took it with him back to the dressing room," Rhonda replied.

The dressing room was in fact one of the church's conference rooms that the show was using as an area to prep its star and guests. Inside were a few tables and mirrors set up for the makeup artist, and a few curtained-off spaces the guests could use to change clothes before the show began taping. This morning Myrtle and I had watched while the makeup artist started to work wonders with my bestie's face. Rhonda was gorgeous anyway, but the makeup made her look ten years younger.

Cindy beamed. "Phew, I'm glad it didn't get damaged. I'll have to borrow it from him so we can film a few teasers to use in the commercials, before he leaves. The producers of *Tussen Kunst en Kitsch* already told me that WWII memorabilia is still an attention-grabber in the Netherlands. And if that kid's granddad was really in the resistance, well, then we have a double-winner."

Rhonda bit her lip. "I hate that what was inside was worth so little."

"The scarf is a disappointment, I'll give you that. But it's the story behind the box that matters, trust me on this."

Rhonda held up her hands. "Don't worry, I know better than to tell you how to do your job. You're the marketing genius, not me."

"Good, I'm glad you agree." Cindy squeezed her arm. "You stay seated until the paramedics arrive, okay?"

Before Rhonda could reply, Cindy rushed back off towards her crew, shouting orders to unplug all of the lamps as she went.

I looked to my friend again, now picking at the glass splinters in her knee.

"Can I just say how proud I am of you? That was a great show!"

"Thank you!" Rhonda beamed up at me.

"I'm sure Myrtle and Sophie are proud of you, too." My words caused her expression to sour again, so I hastened to say, "I know Myrtle's been fangirl'ing you pretty hard, but she means well. She's just intense by nature."

"It's not that. Myrtle's a sweetheart."

My heart sank. "Oh, so it is Lady Sophie. Has something else happened?" She and my partner had started off on the right foot, but during our last mission, they'd stepped on each other's toes something fierce. I thought they'd worked things out since, but based on Rhonda's dark expression, there must still have been bad blood flowing between them.

When Rhonda shook her head, but refused to answer me with words, I added, "You know that Lady Sophie is not upset with you, but pleased that you helped to catch the bad guys." I had noticed that Rhonda had avoided any conversations involving Sophie since they'd seen each other at the last party, two weeks ago. But I figured it had more to do with how the last assignment ended than anything else.

Rhonda only shook her head and dropped her voice. "It's not that. I've researched her tiara."

"That's great! She'll be thrilled to learn anything you've found out about it." In an uncharacteristic moment of openness, the Baroness had admitted to knowing nothing about her favorite family heirloom's history. I knew Rhonda was a little miffed by Sophie's refusal to let her get close, which was why she'd decided to research her tiara as a surprise.

"Oh, I don't know about that. I discovered something she probably doesn't want you to know about. Could we talk about it later, in private?"

I gave my friend a sidelong glance, wanting to ask, but knowing this wasn't the moment to get into it. "Sure, whenever you feel like sharing."

Rhonda opened her mouth to speak again, but apparently thought better of it. She closed her mouth, then waited a minute before asking, "Say, with all the commotion, I forgot to ask. How was the party in Switzerland?"

"To be honest, it was rather boring. Most of the invitees were pretty stiff and stuck-up. It was nothing you would have enjoyed," I reassured her.

My best friend didn't have a clue as to my real job; she still thought that I was a freelancer writing about antiques for the magazine *Hidden Treasures*. The magazine existed, but my articles were all ghostwritten.

"That was the last party on Lady Sophie's social agenda this summer, which means we can have that long weekend at the French Riviera after you finish taping in Amsterdam, if you are still interested."

"That sounds great! Of course I am. I sure am sorry that I ditched you for Julie and the show these past two weeks, but I do appreciate you understanding."

"Of course! You hadn't seen your daughter in ages, and I know that taping a show requires a lot of prep work."

Rhonda reached over and squeezed my arm with her free hand. "You're a doll, you know that? Once we get these first three shows finished, I should be able to take a few days off." She looked down at her knee, thankfully no longer leaking blood. "Assuming this isn't bad enough to warrant a hospital stay."

Before I could respond, a woman yelled out Rhonda's name, causing us both to turn towards the voice's source.

6

Death On Set

"Rhonda Rhodes! Are you alright?" An all-too-familiar voice called out from the wing in which the audience had been sequestered, now cut off from the podium by a row of beefy security guards. During the taping, the men had been positioned by each of the outer doors to ensure the filming was not disrupted. As soon as the electricity went haywire, Cindy had called them in to help contain the crowd. They'd herded the audience members to another section of the church and encouraged everyone to shuffle into the pews and wait for further instructions.

Myrtle was waving with both hands as she yelled out to get our attention. Or, rather, my bestie's eye. I knew she and Reggie were fans of the show, but I'd had no idea just how much they enjoyed it. Since I'd arrived, she'd cornered Rhonda every chance she gotten and interrogated her about objects featured on past shows.

As soon as Rhonda signaled for the security guards to let Myrtle through, she raced over to my bestie. "Damn, that was close. Are you okay?"

Rhonda pursed her lips as she studied my company contact. "You know, with a mouth like that, you'll never make prime time."

"I'll have to remember that, if I ever get asked to be on television." Myrtle ran a hand over her buzz cut, before asking shyly, "Do you think I have what it takes?"

Rhonda studied her critically. "You might just, as long as you keep it clean."

Something about the normalcy of their conversation made me giggle. I could feel the adrenaline starting to dissipate, when another scream pierced the air—one filled with terror and fear. This time, it was coming from behind the curtain.

"What now?" Cindy moaned.

We didn't have to wait long for the answer. A young crew member dressed in black raced through the slit in the curtain and straight into Cindy.

"Dressing room. Jan dead." She leaned over and put her hands on her knees, panting as she did. Before she could catch her breath, I tore off towards the dressing room, my mind refusing to accept the stagehand's words at face value. As I raced towards the hallway and past the bathrooms, I noted Cindy and Theresa were at my heels. Yet when I reached the dressing room door, the sight before me stopped me dead in my tracks.

Sure enough, the young man was no longer with us. My best guess was that he'd fallen hard against the edge of the dressing room table, its corner now streaked with red, before sliding onto the floor and onto his side. Jan's eyes were rolled back, and his chest didn't move a millimeter. It probably had something to do with the stream of blood flowing out of the back of his head. More disturbing was the expression of pure confusion on Jan's face.

I forced myself not to stare into his dead face for too long, but to examine the rest of the scene, at least with my eyes. The puzzle box his granddad had made lay on the floor close to his feet. However, the scarf he'd been clutching in his hands when he left the stage was no longer wrapped up in his grip. From a quick scan of the room, I didn't see it anywhere.

Apparently, I wasn't the only one who noticed. Several of the crew members were now crowding around the door, too. Theresa, Cindy's assistant, gasped loudly from behind me. "Look—the scarf is missing! Why would anyone kill that poor sweet boy for an ugly scarf?"

The rest gasped right along with her.

"And his wallet is still on the dressing table, next to his iPhone. That's the newest model. Why would a thief leave that behind?" Cindy asked.

I held onto the doorframe and leaned inside, almost afraid to actually enter the space. As an art sleuth, I was used to finding myself in compromising positions and even breaking the law. But dealing with dead bodies was not part of my typical workday, and corpses still gave me the jitters.

More crew members pushed behind me, straining to look inside. Yet I wasn't quite ready to step aside. My eyes swept over the rest of the room, noting that Jan had removed his jacket and hung it up on a coat hook by the door. If he was killed for the artwork, the letters he'd had in his pocket may shed some light as to why someone had killed him, or even reveal their identity. Jan had mentioned that his granddad wrote about having hidden art away. If that was true, those letters would be worth reading.

A large man pushed forward through the small group of crew members and then around Cindy, until he'd reached me, still half-hanging inside the doorframe. It was the operator with camera troubles, I realized. "Did someone kill the kid?"

"It sure looks like it," I muttered.

When the cameraman began to step around me to get a better look at the body, Cindy's shrieks stopped him in his tracks.

"Joris—stop right there! No one goes inside! We have to call the police. This is a crime scene." Her words caught in her throat, and she dropped her head into her hands. "That poor kid."

Then, as suddenly as she'd begun crying, she stopped and straightened up. "Everyone, back to the podium. Anton—has anyone called the police yet?" She herded the small group of crew members back towards the stage, calling out to her director as she went.

Knowing this might be the only time I had to examine the crime scene, I dragged my feet. As soon as the last of the group was out of sight, I pulled a tissue out of my purse, then leaned into the dressing room and felt inside Jan's jacket pocket. Sure enough, the letters were still inside. Using the tissue, I pulled the pile out and quickly removed the first from its envelope.

The sight made me sigh. Of course, they were written in Dutch. Which meant I would either need to find a translator willing to be discreet, or use an online tool and take my chances that the translation was accurate. But for now, I could at least take photos of them all. I was certain that once the police arrived, they wouldn't let me anywhere near this dressing room, even if I told them who I really worked for.

It only took a minute to snap shots of all six letters. They were thankfully brief and, more importantly, written in a neat handwriting, which would make them infinitely easier to translate. When Theresa came back to look for me, I had already popped them back into Jan's pocket and was walking towards the podium.

When she glared at me and crossed her arms over her torso, I shrugged and nodded towards the ladies' room. "Sorry, I had to use the restroom."

Theresa pursed her lips a moment, but soon nodded instead. "Cindy wants everyone to stay together, just in case there's still a madman hiding out in the church somewhere."

Her words stopped me in my tracks. "Madman? Whoever killed Jan has to be someone working on the show or in the audience. If anyone had opened an outside door, we would have noticed the light streaming in. Besides, there were security guards stationed at each entrance, so that no one could interrupt the taping."

Theresa's mouth formed an O, and her face drained of color. "That means one of us is a killer!"

She raced back to Cindy, screaming as she went. She was still weeping when I caught up to them.

"What did you say to Theresa? She's inconsolable," Cindy spat as soon as she noticed me approaching.

"The truth—that whoever did this to Jan was either a member of the crew or audience. No one else had access to the space during filming. The security personnel stationed outside each of the outer doors ensured that."

Cindy paled as the truth of my words sank in. Before she could react, the front door to the church opened, and police officers began streaming inside.

I watched as a beefy security agent led a gaggle of officers into the church and over to Cindy. Moments later, a team of paramedics rushed through with a stretcher. When Cindy led them to the dressing room, I wanted to tell them to slow down, knowing there was no reason for them to run. Jan was beyond saving.

"Carmen! What's going on? Is Jan really dead?" Rhonda called out. I crossed over to her, while still watching as several agents got to work setting up tables in the same wing where the audience had been confined, I assumed to question all present.

"Well, are you going to tell us, or do we have to guess?" Myrtle groused.

"Sorry, right, here's what happened…" As I briefed them, my bestie's expression became increasingly more stricken.

"That poor boy. What a shame." Rhonda looked to the puzzle box on the table. "They killed Jan for the scarf? Is that what you're saying?"

I nodded. "It sure looks like it. It's the darndest thing, but the only thing that appears to be missing from the room was that worthless scarf. His grandfather's letters are still in his jacket pocket. They even left his wallet and phone behind, and it was an expensive model."

"That doesn't make any sense." Rhonda shook her head. I knew it was going to take her a few minutes to accept the facts.

"What concerns me more right now is, who would kill anyone to get ahold of that ugly thing? We can figure out the why later. From what I could tell, the only possible candidates were the crew and audience members present at today's taping. And considering one would have had to walk alongside the podium to get backstage, that limits the suspect list to the crew, as far as I am concerned."

"Why do you say that?" Myrtle asked.

"Jan walked back to the dressing room moments before the lights went out. I bet whoever shorted out the power did so intentionally so they could kill him under the cover of darkness."

Myrtle and Rhonda grew quiet.

"Which means it must have been planned," I added when they did not say anything. "But when and by whom? Did they know what was hidden inside that box? And if they were after the scarf, how did they find out about it?"

"If someone knew that there was something hidden inside that box, then all they had to do was turn on the television yesterday, and they would have known where to find it. Cindy said there were lots of advertisements for the show featuring Jan's puzzle box."

"But that would mean that they planned this quite quickly, if it was only aired on Dutch television yesterday."

"I guess it does. Say, Myrtle, can I talk to you for a moment?"

I pulled her aside and out of Rhonda's hearing range before my bestie could protest. I leaned in towards Myrtle's ear, keeping my voice soft.

"I know the Dutch police are going to investigate Jan's death, but I would feel a whole lot better if Rosewood and Interpol got involved, too. I know it appears that the scarf is what they were after, but if Rhonda is in any sort of danger, I would never forgive myself for not helping to get this investigation wrapped up as soon as possible."

"I agree completely, which is why I've already called Reggie. Anything we need to solve this, we are authorized to use."

I felt a wave of relief flowing over me. "That's great. Let me call Dave and see if he can get Interpol involved."

"There's no need. Reggie's already discussed it with Dave's boss. Since that last case, they've been in close contact, which is good for both agencies. Because Jan's attacker seemed to be after a cultural artifact, Dave's team is authorized to help out. And his boss said he knew of the perfect agent for the job. It's not Dave because he's out on another assignment, but it is a member of his team. Her name escapes me right now, but she is already on her way to Amsterdam and will get in touch with me whenever she arrives."

"Some cultural object. That has to be the ugliest scarf I've ever seen." I kicked an imaginary pebble with my shoe, wondering why I was disappointed that Dave would not be assigned to the case, considering I was the one who wasn't interested in pursuing a relationship with him right now.

"That's neither here nor there. It must be important for one reason or another, otherwise it wouldn't have been stolen."

"True. Could you SMS me the Interpol agent's telephone number?"

"You bet. But let's assume it was a simple theft gone wrong and that it had nothing to do with Rhonda until we find evidence proving otherwise, okay?"

I bit my lip, knowing she was right, but still frustrated that a man had been killed and the scarf stolen during my friend's show, mere feet from where I was now standing, and I had been helpless to do anything about it.

7

Investigation Time

As I looked over at the small team of cameramen, stagehands, and directors, I felt a knot forming in my stomach. Whoever killed Jan was someone working closely with my bestie. And that meant I needed to get myself involved in this investigation. If I couldn't be a part of it officially, I could at least eavesdrop on the police interviews. There were enough people milling about that me pretending to check my phone for messages wouldn't seem out of place.

I took in the placement of the foldup tables, realizing they were close enough to the pews that I could listen in on one or two interviews at once. Yet before I could position myself in the pew closest to the tables, Rhonda piped up.

"Wait a second—Carmen, why exactly do you know that the letters are still in his pocket? You weren't snooping around in the dressing room after his death, were you? The last thing we need is for the police to find your fingerprints in there."

I ticked my tongue against my teeth. "I was careful, and I only removed them long enough to photograph them, before I put them back. If what he said was true about his granddad hiding artwork away, they might provide a clue as to why that scarf is worth killing for."

"May I have everyone's attention?" An older man in uniform spoke up, effectively cutting off the many conversations buzzing around the room. "I am Detective Philip De Rijke of the Amsterdam police force. A crime has been committed here, and we need to interview everyone present before we can release any of you. Considering the sheer number of people present, it may take us a few hours, so I ask now for your understanding. I have six officers available to take your statements. Please have your identification ready when we call you over. Thank you."

He immediately began waving the audience members closest to him over to the tables and awaiting officers. Considering there were about a hundred audience members and another twenty or so crew members, it was going to take a while. Which was fine as far as I was concerned because it gave me a chance to gather a few clues and perhaps even interview a few suspects of my own.

"I'm going to hang around the tables and see what I can overhear. Good luck." Myrtle set off before either Rhonda or I could respond. I was glad to see that my company contact had the same idea that I'd had.

Yet before I could join her, I noticed Rhonda's knee was leaking blood again. "Hon, we really need a paramedic to look at that."

I spotted the paramedics that Cindy had called and gestured them over to my bestie before she could refuse. Quite soon, a young paramedic was pulling shards of glass out of her knee with a large set of tweezers. Her grimace made clear that it wasn't pleasant, but I was thrilled to hear that she wouldn't have to be hospitalized because of it.

While the medic was busy with his patient, I decided to let Myrtle deal with the interviews while I took a quick look at the letters. I plopped down onto the chair across from Rhonda on the podium and opened the photos on my phone, holding it so that no one could easily see what I was looking at. However, my time was wasted, I feared. The letters were long enough that I would need to transcribe the Dutch text into my telephone first and then feed that through an online translator. Doing that here, while surrounded by police officers actively searching for a clue as to the young man's killer, didn't seem like the smartest move. I had no desire to explain to them how I had gotten ahold of a copy of Jan's grandfather's letters. Which meant I would need to wait and do this back at the hotel or find someone discreet who would be willing to translate these for me, instead.

When I looked up, Rhonda's knee was neatly bandaged, and the paramedic was cleaning up his gear. After he left his patient with a bottle of painkillers, Rhonda nodded to my phone. "Have you found out anything from those letters yet?"

I glanced around, relieved to see that no officers were close by. "I'm afraid not; they're in Dutch, too. So we'll either need to ask someone to help translate them, or take our chances with an online translation tool."

Rhonda frowned. "Those online tools can be so unreliable, I don't know if we could trust the translations. I would rather ask a human. Why don't we ask Theresa, Cindy's assistant, to suggest someone? She's pretty helpful and seems to know everyone."

"Great idea. I don't want to upset that paramedic so why don't you remain seated so you can keep the pressure off of your knee. If Theresa suggests someone who can help us, I'll ask them to come over here, so you can hear what they say. Alright?"

"That's great, thanks. To be honest, I'm glad to stay put. The painkillers are kicking in, and I'm feeling pretty lightheaded."

I squeezed her shoulder. "I'll be right back. Hang tight."

It took me a minute to find Theresa because she was scrunched down low in a pew, scrolling through photos on her phone. "Hey, Theresa, how are you doing?"

She perked up at her name. "Hi. It's Carmen, right? You're Rhonda's old friend."

I chuckled. "Well, we have been friends since we were kids, so I guess that makes me an old friend."

Theresa blushed. "Sorry, I didn't mean to be disrespectful."

"Of course not." I nodded at a photo open on her phone, of the canals of Amsterdam at sunset. "Wow, that's a gorgeous photo. You've got a great eye for composition."

"Thanks! Photography is my hobby. It's been wonderful to have new subject matter."

When she pushed a wisp of hair back over her ear, her bracelet rolled forward over her wrist. I took in the large, silver-plated charms, each of a monument in Europe.

I studied the tiny Eiffel Tower, Roman Coliseum, London's Big Ben, and a Dutch windmill with a rotating blade, among others. It was slightly childish, but each charm was so well-made, it was fascinating. "That's a pretty impressive charm bracelet."

"Thanks, it was a gift from my sister. It's all the places I said I wanted to visit someday. It's been a dream of mine to travel the world. That's why I studied travel and tourism, but it just never happened—until now, that is."

"Gosh, travel and tourism sounds exciting, but quite different than working in television. How did you end up working for *Antiques Time*?"

Theresa's lips pursed. "Yeah, well, I graduated right as the coronavirus shut down the world, making my diploma utterly useless. A friend knew somebody who knew Cindy, and they got me an interview. Technically I'm her assistant, but really I'm just here to herd the stagehands and get her coffee. There's not much more to it."

"How are you enjoying Europe so far?"

"It's great!" She beamed, before chewing on her lower lip. "I mean, besides that young man being murdered. I've never been able to travel, given my salary and student debt. My sister's pretty upset that I missed her wedding, but once she's calmed down, she'll realize that this was a chance of a lifetime that I just couldn't pass up."

"That's great. I hope you get some free time to see more of the cities you are filming in."

"We will. At least Cindy promised us all at least one free day in each city, depending on how fast we can get the next round of appraisal days organized."

I nodded enthusiastically, then changed the subject. "Say, listen, I was wondering if you could help me out with something. I'm hoping one of the local crew members might be able to help me translate Dutch letters into English, and wondered if you had a suggestion as to who I should approach."

"Oh, gosh, any of the crew, I suspect. Let me think who would be the best one for this job." She tapped on her chin and her eyes shot to the right. But before she could come up with the answer, an officer waved her over.

"Golly, it's my turn to be interviewed. I'll get you a name as soon as I'm done, alright?"

She skipped over to the little table to be interviewed, leaving me to return to Rhonda empty-handed.

"We'll have to wait until her interview is over. Maybe we could ask Cindy."

Rhonda grimaced. "She's got so much on her plate right now. I would hate to bother her with this."

"I can translate the letters for you," a heavily accented voice offered from behind.

I whipped around to see one of the cameramen standing quite close. "I heard you talking to Theresa. I can translate them from Dutch to English, if you want."

"Oh, that would be great, actually. You sure you don't mind?"

"Not at all. The police have already interviewed me, and I'm already bored sitting around waiting to leave. This will give me something to do. I'd be happy to help."

I looked to Rhonda and raised my eyebrows. "Sure, I mean, great—and thanks…" I looked up at him blankly.

"Joris Smit." The large man held out his hand.

"How long will it take you to translate them?"

Joris chuckled. "I suppose I would need to know how many there are and how long each one is, before I could tell you for certain. But why don't we start with, whose letters are they?"

I glanced around to ensure no one was close enough to hear me. "There are six letters written during World War II, the ones that Jan's granddad wrote. The same ones Jan brought to the taping and mentioned during the show. I have photos of them that I can send to you."

His whole face lit up at the mention of the war. "Then I'm your man. My granddad was in the resistance during the war and told me so many stories about his experiences that I sometimes feel like I lived through it, too. But how did you…" His voice trailed off as his eyes widened to saucers. It was as if he finally put two and two together.

When he locked eyes with me, his expression was a mixture of fear and fascination. "Did you hurt Jan?"

"God, no! I didn't kill him! I took photographs of the letters after his death. They are still in his jacket pocket, the same one that's hanging next to the door."

Joris studied my face, as if he was trying to discern whether I was telling the truth, before slowly nodding. "Alright. Send them over."

He pulled out his phone, and we exchanged numbers. A few clicks later and he had all of the letters.

"Could you give me a few minutes to study them, to put all of the information in context first, before I translate them for you?"

"Certainly. Give us a shout whenever you're ready."

"Will do." He sat down on one of the chairs on the podium and took his time reading the text.

I scanned the room, figuring this was as good a time as any to try to find Cindy and see what she thought of her crew. If my presumption was correct, one of them was a killer. If Cindy had noticed one of them acting suspicious, I wanted to confront them now, before the police released us all. I soon spotted her in one corner, sitting in a pew with her hands over her face. I could only imagine what a nightmare this filming had turned into for her. Nevertheless, I had a murder to solve.

8

Questioning Cindy

Cindy whipped her head up as I approached. The fierceness of her expression startled me, but thankfully her menacing glare softened into a smile quite quickly. "Oh, Carmen, it's you. I was afraid the police had more questions for me. Right now, I don't seem to have the right answers to any of them."

"It truly is a nightmare. How are you holding up?"

"Better than Jan Mank, so that's something." Cindy ran her hand over her face. "Sorry, that was inappropriate. I'm okay, just ready to go back to my hotel room and take a hot bath. But by the looks of things, it's going to be a while before any of us are released."

"Rhonda and I were wondering if the police had discovered anything new."

She snorted. "You could say that. They found a nail topped with a cork, jammed into a socket in the hallway, between the bathrooms and our studio setup. Someone intentionally caused the power to surge so that the lights would go out."

I nodded before finishing her thought. "Which means whoever caused the power to go out is probably our killer."

"Exactly." Cindy dipped her head. "I hope it's someone in the audience, because I can't believe any of my crew did this."

I sat down next to her, glad she had broached the subject herself. "How well do you know them, anyway?"

Cindy cocked her head, apparently considering my question. "Honestly,

I don't know the local crew that well, save for working with them the past week while getting the stage set up. But they seem like an enthusiastic group, and they have all worked for the Dutch program *Tussen Kunst en Kitsch*, so they are all familiar with antiques and collectibles. I couldn't imagine that any of them would suddenly decide to steal something now, and especially not that scarf."

I had trouble hiding my disappointment. She had a good point about the chances that a crew member used to being around valuable antiques would decide to steal the scarf, of all things. "Okay, well…"

Cindy's eyes shot to the left. "Wait, that's not completely true. Anton Berhard is a last minute fill-in. The director we'd hired got food poisoning the day before we shot the first show and had to bow out. She recommended Anton, and he was available, so he got the job."

"What do you think of him?"

The way she narrowed her eyes and paused to consider her words made me suspicious. "Well, he's hard to peg. He seems to think he's too good for this gig, but his resume is pretty flimsy, so I'm not certain why he thinks that."

"What do you mean? Could you give me an example?"

"It's hard to explain, I guess it's more of a feeling than anything else." Cindy bit her lip for a moment, before suddenly continuing, "Okay, here's one. Instead of picking up where my original director had left off, Anton immediately decided to make the show his own. Which would be fine under normal circumstances, but we had already spent a week hashing everything out, and we were hours away from taping a live show. So when he changed the lighting and the framing for two of the camera angles, I explained why we'd done what we'd done, and asked him to change them back. But instead of talking it out with me, he flew off the handle and demanded that his changes be implemented or he was walking off the show."

"Oof, he sounds like a prima donna," I whispered.

Cindy nodded furiously. "Precisely. That was not the right moment to mess with things, and he should have been professional enough to know that. However, I had no other options, so I let him use his camera framing and lighting. It's quite a bit more dramatic than I would have preferred, but it works."

"And what about your camera people, like Joris?"

Cindy laughed. "You don't have to be politically correct—they are all male."

"Fair enough. What do you think of them?"

"Joris is quite the charmer. His English is impeccable and he's helpful and friendly, too. I trust him, perhaps more than the other two cameramen. They seem professional enough, but aren't very sociable so I haven't been able to get a handle on their personalities."

I nodded, feeling the same about Joris, even though I'd only met him a few minutes earlier.

"And the stagehands?"

"Gosh, I honestly don't have much to do with them—that's Theresa's department. But I haven't heard her complaining about anyone not pulling their weight."

"And what about Theresa?"

Cindy locked eyes with me. "What about her? You don't think she has anything to do with this—do you? She's been my assistant for years and missed her sister's wedding to help me film these European shows. I trust her implicitly."

I held up my hands to ward off her glare. "Okay, I get it. Theresa is above board."

"Yes, she is. Now is there anything else you need? I want to check in with the police and see if they know when we can leave." Cindy rose and began to storm off, only to pause midstep and glance back at me. "Have you been interviewed yet?"

"No, not yet."

She rolled her eyes and blew out her cheeks. "We're in for a long day, aren't we?"

9

Translating The Letters

When I stood, wondering whether to try to sneak into the dressing room to look for clues or eavesdrop on other crew members' whispered conversations, Joris waved me back over.

As I walked closer, I could tell he was bubbling with excitement, which got me excited as well. "So, what have you discovered?"

When I plopped down next to him, he leaned in towards me, a wide smile on his face. "These do seem to be written by Jan's grandfather. It sounds like he wrote these to his son during the war. For a WWII buff like me, they are fascinating to read through. But most of it is about daily life and the grandfather's longing to be reunited with his son, Jan's father. Though I can't tell whether they were actually delivered to Jan's father or whether they were found after the war ended. I can say that there are a few interesting details that don't quite make sense, especially in the last letter. Maybe those are the clues you are looking for."

I narrowed my eyes at my best friend, who looked away and blushed. Oh great, Miss Indiscretion had probably told Joris everything about why we were interested in translating these. She really would not make a good art sleuth, no matter what her connections may be. I would have to make a conversation with Reggie about Rhonda a priority.

Joris glanced down at his phone. "Shall I dictate the letters to you in English? That might be the fastest way. Though I should warn you, much of it is pretty mundane."

"That would be great—thank you. And as far as I'm concerned, you can summarize the more boring bits and skip to the interesting parts."

"Alright. There are six letters, spaced a few months apart. In the first two, the grandfather is hoping that his son is being treated well by their distant relatives; he is saddened that they have to be apart for so long and he can't wait for the war to end. In the third, he seems to realize that the war won't be ending soon. That's when he begins to tell his son more about his work for the resistance group, the Klavers. His references are vague and guarded, but I recognize them from my granddad's stories."

Joris looked up at us. "My granddad was also in the resistance, but his group was more involved in destroying city records than saving cultural treasures. But he told me all about the actions his group took part in and several others that were active at the time—including the Klavers. I recall that he had quite a bit of respect for their work. They were quite successful at moving both people and their valuables to the south and were famous for their daring actions. Granddad said they'd even blown up a bridge once, to hinder their German pursuers. It is fascinating to read about their work, from the perspective of one of their members."

"I can imagine," I murmured, wondering what to note down. So far, I hadn't heard anything new. When I looked back up, he had swiped to the photo of another letter.

"Jan had mentioned on the show that his granddad was afraid of someone. In this last letter, he clearly states that he had discovered there was a small group of what he calls 'bad seeds'—profiteers posing as resistance members—who had infiltrated their organization. They had been stealing crates filled with the art and antiques entrusted to them, instead of transporting them to the underground bunkers the group had been using in the south."

"That's right. Jan did mention them during the taping this morning," Rhonda confirmed.

"The grandfather even names three of the bad seeds in this letter," the cameraman rushed to add.

His words made me sit up a little straighter. "Really? We should give their names to the police and see what they can find out about the families. The men are probably dead by now, but there's always a chance their relatives are involved, somehow."

"Great thinking, Carmen," Rhonda beamed.

Joris nodded in agreement. "But there's more to tell. It sounds like the grandfather had stolen one shipment back from them and had hidden it away before he penned this last letter. He writes that he left his son a special puzzle box in their secret space at home, and that he should treasure it. But I don't see any direct mention of where he had hidden the artwork, or where exactly that secret space was located. The letter is dated May 8, 1940. Jan did say his granddad was killed right after the war ended."

I locked eyes with Joris. "That might be why the granddad was killed—because of the art he'd stolen. Especially if those bad seeds tracked him down and demanded the art's return."

"They must not have found it if Jan still had the puzzle box," Joris added.

"Oh my—does that mean that the box will lead us to the art?" Rhonda exclaimed so loudly, I wanted to clamp my hand over her mouth.

"Maybe, but how? There was only a badly knit scarf inside," I said in a soft voice.

"Why didn't the son open the box and follow the trail?" Rhonda groused.

"Now that Jan is dead, I suppose we will never know. But he did mention on the show that his dad was depressed and teared up at the mere mention of his father. Maybe he just couldn't face his past and never dared to open it?" I suggested.

"That might be so. Grief and depression can do strange things to one's mind," Rhonda said.

I thought back to how I felt after my Carlos had been killed, and how grief-stricken and confused I had been for months on end. I could imagine how he would rather not have opened the box, that its mere existence would be something he would avoid confronting, as well as what it may have led to.

Joris seemed to be as frustrated as we were. "Just so you know, there is no mention of this specific puzzle box. Maybe this one doesn't have anything to do with the location of the artwork, after all. The granddad could have meant another box, or maybe he meant something else altogether. 'The box' might be a code word that only his son would have understood."

"I'm afraid you're right, it could be any of the three." I sighed, uncertain as to what to do next. "Rhonda, did the grandson mention where he'd found the puzzle box?"

My bestie shook her head. "No, unfortunately he did not. Only that he'd found several crates of his grandfather's things, after his dad died. He'd brought this one to the show because he thought it was the most expensive-looking one."

I snapped my fingers. "All may not be lost quite yet. We still have the three names Jan's grandfather mentioned in his letter. What if one of their relatives is here, in the audience?"

Rhonda shot up. "We really have to share these names with the police!"

I stood and straightened my jacket. "You're right. I haven't had my interview yet. Let me see if the police can talk to me now."

When I looked over at the men in uniform, Joris hung his head. "Sorry I couldn't help more."

I grabbed his arm, surprised at how hard his bicep was. "Oh, no, you've been a huge help. Thanks again."

"Sure, and if you have any more questions about WWII history or the resistance groups, feel free to give me a call. You have my number."

"We sure will." I nodded my head vigorously, fairly certain it wouldn't be necessary to involve him further, but appreciating his offer, nonetheless.

10

Getting To Know The Crew

When I began to walk towards the interview tables, I noted Myrtle coming towards me at high speed, a smirk on her face. "It might not be the crew after all. One of the cameramen saw an audience member sneaking around backstage just before the lights went out."

"How do you know that? All of my interviews were in Dutch."

"One of the stagehands is Spanish, and the others were catching him up on what they'd overheard so far."

"That's handy."

"It is. That cameraman's statement means that we have to consider everyone present, not just the crew, which means we have many more suspects to sift through."

I sighed. "I suppose you're right. One of the crew offered to translate the letters for us, a guy named Joris. He just confirmed for us that Jan's grandfather named three of the bad seeds in his letters. I'm going to share them with the police now. Maybe that will help them narrow down the suspect list."

"Excellent. Which one is Joris?"

When I pointed him out, she gasped. "Wait a second, I think that's the cameraman they were referring to. Did you question him about what he'd seen?"

"No, we were only discussing the letters."

"Well, why don't we go talk to him now and find out what he saw exactly."

Myrtle rushed over to Joris before I could respond. I trailed after her, hoping she would go easy on him. He'd generously translated the letters for us, without asking for anything in return. I hoped her somewhat abrasive personality wouldn't put him off.

Yet before I could catch up, Myrtle was already in full interrogation mode. "Did you tell the police that you saw someone moving towards the backstage area, shortly before the lights went out?" Myrtle asked in a way that made clear she expected a straight answer.

"I did, but I didn't get a good look at them because the director approached me and distracted me. By the time we were finished, I didn't see the person anymore. But I did notice that there was an empty chair on the left side of the audience."

I leaned back on one heel. "What did the director want from you during a shoot? That seems like a bad time to chat."

"My camera's feed to the monitor was cutting out, and he couldn't tell if my camera was recording or not. But in order to recalibrate it, I would have had to shut the camera down. Since we were almost done taping the show, he decided to turn off my feed and use the other cameras, instead."

"And was your camera recording properly?" Myrtle demanded.

He scratched at his chin. "I honestly do not know. I followed Anton behind the curtain and then joined Cindy at the monitor bay, but the electricity cut out before we could check the feed."

"Wait—didn't Anton return to the monitors?"

"No, he headed straight towards the bathroom. He's got quite the temper and was pretty angry about my camera cutting out. I figured he needed a minute to compose himself."

I nodded my head slowly as I processed what Joris had said. If Anton was in the bathroom, he was right next to the dressing room. I kept my face passive, yet knew Anton was now a person of interest. Instead of asking about his whereabouts, I tried another tactic.

"That wasn't very professional of him to be away from the monitors so long. He is the director, after all."

Joris snorted. "Professional is not a term I would use to describe Anton. He's made it clear from the moment he arrived that he sees himself as a documentary filmmaker, not a television director, and is only doing this gig as a favor to a friend. I hoped the other director would have recovered in time for the taping, because she was great to work with. But this guy clearly thinks that television, as a medium, is beneath him."

"Thanks for the clarification." Myrtle slapped him on the shoulder.

"Interesting. Thanks, Joris."

"Anytime." He tipped his head before joining the crew again.

My mind raced with possibilities. We had a mysterious guest and an angry director wandering around where they shouldn't have been, moments before the murder. Before I could puzzle out the implications, Myrtle lay her hand on my shoulder.

"I'm going to go check on Rhonda."

"Great, I'll be over as soon as I've talked to the police."

"See you soon."

Knowing my bestie was in good hands, I set off to share my intel with the local police force. Yet when I strode over to the nearest officer and asked to be interviewed, he merely pointed to a pew full of audience members still waiting to speak with an agent. When I protested, arguing that I had important information to share, the agent's tired expression didn't waver. So I reluctantly took my place, tapping my foot in protest. With nothing to do but wait, I decided to listen in on the other interviews.

Quite soon, I realized that I was not going to learn much; almost all of the crew members were Dutch, so I couldn't really follow along word for word. Yet based on the speed of the questions flying across the table, and the passive expressions of the officers writing things down, it seemed that the police were in a hurry to get everyone's statements but not yet interested in dealing with the information presented. I couldn't blame them; there were still a few dozen people to interview, and many were already grumbling about having to stay until everyone had been questioned.

I lucked out when Theresa, Cindy's American assistant, was called over. I leaned forward, eager to hear her answers to the police's questions. She responded in a flat voice, instead of her usual sparkly one, I presumed out of respect for the dead.

I didn't learn anything new, until the officer asked whether she'd seen an audience member backstage.

"I don't question what that cameraman said, but I was by the monitor bay and focused on the taping the entire time. I didn't notice anyone sneaking around."

That's odd, I thought. I'd seen her scurrying about during the show, not standing still.

After a few more perfunctory questions, Theresa was excused, and Cindy was called back over.

"I told you before, I didn't see anyone out of place. Anton and I were in front of the monitors, standing with our backs to the hallway and headphones on, for the entire show." From her snippy tone, it was obvious that she was not pleased to be questioned again.

The officer cocked his head at her. "Are you certain? We've had several witnesses mention an audience member walking around just before the blackout."

"I don't know anything about that," Cindy said. "The only odd thing that I noticed during the taping was the monitor for camera two cutting out towards the end of the taping. That's why Anton stepped out to check the cables. But there was nothing we could do about it while we were taping, so he returned to the monitor bay, and we were wrapping up the show when the electricity went out."

The officer noted her response, as did I, before asking Cindy another string of questions about the stagehand's movements. Her curt responses made clear that she had nothing new to add. When she got up from the table, Cindy looked even more haggard.

The police interviewed several more audience members, thankfully some English-speaking, who also reported seeing someone get up from their seat right before the lights went out. Yet, just as many asserted that no one got up.

I was beginning to feel sorry for the police. With so many witnesses and no video evidence to help them, they were going to have a heck of a time sorting out the truth.

My interest began to wane when several Dutch speakers were interviewed in a row. That is, until Anton was waved over. I'd noticed him tapping his knee and grumbling to himself as he waited on the pew for it to be his turn. By the time he sat across from the officer, it was clear that he was fuming mad because he'd been made to wait so long.

I sat up a little straighter to ensure that I could see all he'd said. Despite the language barrier, his posturing and snippy tone made clear that Anton was offended and acting defensive all at the same time. I knew, from what Cindy and Joris had said, that he thought himself a documentary filmmaker, not a television maker.

I opened my phone to use the translate function to try to follow their conversation, but before I could, another officer waved me over to his table.

11

Interviewing Carmen

Being summoned now by the police, right as Anton's interview got heated, was probably for the best. The online translation tools I had used in the past were often wrong, and it wouldn't do to be misled by an app. Besides, it was time to inform the police about the bad seeds.

The officers stuck behind the tables looked exhausted. Considering we'd been trapped here for several hours, they all had my sympathy. As I sat down at my assigned place, the policeman across from me removed the questionnaire-style report he'd apparently just filled in during his last interview, and grabbed a new, clean sheet. On it were about ten questions preprinted on a single page. Reading letters upside down was a skill I had acquired long ago, but in this case, it was useless. Since the questions were in Dutch, I would have to wait to hear how the officer translated them.

The policeman across from me was quite direct, and his questions convinced me that they were more interested in gathering information than investigating at this point. And who could blame them? They had around one hundred interviews to conduct, and would have to spend days on the arduous task of compiling all of the information into one comprehensive timeline.

I answered his questions as best I could, waiting for my chance to share my intel. However, once he'd come to the end of his question list, he seemed ready to dismiss me.

When he looked over at the pews filled with those still waiting to be interviewed, I leaned forward, blocking his view. "I do have one more thing to add that may help your investigation."

He threw his pen onto the clipboard and folded his hands in front of him. "Shoot."

When I told him about Jan mentioning on the show that his grandfather named several 'bad seeds' in his letters, and about the possibility that the three men named in his last letter may have killed him, he seemed genuinely interested.

"We found the letters you mention in Jan Mank's jacket pocket. One of my colleagues is reading through them now. Knowing that Jan's grandfather may have been killed by one of them is important information. I'll pass it along."

"And will you check to see if any of their relatives might be in the audience?"

"That goes without saying."

"It may be that one of their relatives came to this show to get ahold of the box," I added, a little too eagerly for someone pretending to be nothing more than a concerned citizen. As tempting as it was to reveal my true identity and insert myself into the investigation, I knew from past experience that exposing my true motives and employer's name sometimes made me a person of interest—something I wished to avoid at all costs. As much as I wanted to tell him that the three names were in the last letter, I would have to admit to having removed the letters from Jan's jacket after his death and photographing them, before replacing them. So I had to let the investigation run its course and hope the officer reading the letters soon found the bad seeds' names.

Yet, before I left the desk, I had one more item to share. "Based on what Jan shared with the show's host, it sounded like that box somehow leads to a treasure trove of artwork. It's worth pursuing, don't you think?"

The officer's mask of weariness returned. "Others have mentioned that possibility, but at this point in the investigation, we are more concerned about finding this young man's murderer than going on a treasure hunt."

"But what if he was killed because of whatever the grandfather had hidden away?"

"Lady, you don't even know for certain that the grandfather did hide something away. When we find his killer, we'll ask about the box, okay?"

It was clear that the officer was only interested in the murder, not the possibility that the puzzle box might lead to something more. As far as I was concerned, that was a green light to investigate further. "Alright then, good luck with your investigation."

12

Stealing The Box

As soon as I scurried back over to my company contact and bestie, I whispered, "Ladies, the police are only interested in the murder, not in the possibility that the puzzle box might somehow lead to a treasure trove of stolen art. Yet, if the granddad did bury something away, I bet it is the reason he was killed."

"That very well could be," Rhonda cried.

"I'm going to get that box. There might be another clue inside. You didn't look for another opening, did you?"

"No, in fact I did not. And you are right, it is possible that there were multiple hiding spots in that one. It is quite large. But you can't tamper with a crime scene!"

"I wouldn't have to tamper if the police were willing to follow the trail of clues presented," I snapped. "You and Myrtle stay here, okay? If you see any agents heading towards the dressing room, maybe you can make a scene of some kind, to draw attention to yourself, instead."

Rhonda dabbed at her forehead. "Oh, lordy, I hope you hurry."

I slipped behind the curtain and walked past the monitor bay towards the hallway. Because the toilets were back here, I had a legitimate excuse to be in the hallway. But not the dressing room, located around the corner from the restrooms.

Using the balls of my feet, I made my way as quietly as I could down the hallway and towards the dressing room. I didn't hear any voices or footsteps behind me, so I grew bolder in my actions, and ended up walking straight through the open door. The police hadn't even taped off the space. The body was gone, thankfully; otherwise I wouldn't have dared to enter.

Initially, I was surprised that the space had been left unguarded, but upon further inspection, I realized there was nothing valuable in here worth guarding. Doing so would have been a waste of manpower, and they needed every available officer interviewing potential witnesses. It was simply a space for the crew to store their jackets, and the makeup artist to prepare the guests for the show. The puzzle box was the only antique in here, and it wasn't worth enough that a normal person would try to steal it in order to resell it.

It was still on the ground but no longer on its side. The white powder covering its surface told me that the police had already dusted it for fingerprints. As silly as it seemed, I couldn't shake the feeling that it was still important, somehow, and that I needed to take it with me.

I felt terrible stealing potential evidence, but consoled myself with the thought that I could always return it later. Only once I had it in my hand did I realize that it was far too big to fit into my clutch purse. I scanned the space for a bag or carry-all to hide it in, but nothing in the room seemed to be large enough. With no alternative, I took off my jacket and draped it over the arm I held the box in. If I didn't whip around too quickly, the coat should cover the box long enough to sneak it into Rhonda's massive tote bag, currently on the podium next to its owner.

A troubling thought crossed my mind. Had the killer only left the box behind because it was too large to hide? If that was the case, they were probably planning on coming back later to claim it. Yet if they did find it missing, they wouldn't know where to look for it, I reasoned.

I exited the dressing room and was rounding the corner to the bathrooms when Anton stormed in.

"What were you doing in the dressing room?" Anton asked as he stepped in front of me, blocking my path back to the podium.

"I wasn't in there, I was using the bathroom," I snapped back.

When he seemed to express an unusual interest in my jacket, I tried to spread out my coat further over the box, without drawing attention to my actions. He must have seen what I was doing, for he smirked. "What's under your jacket?"

I ignored him and stepped forward, but he didn't move aside. So I tried another tactic. "Why did you interrupt the cameraman during the live show?"

He stopped staring at my jacket and glared up at me, instead, as I hoped he would. "I wasn't interrupting him. His camera's feed was cutting out, and I was trying to figure out why."

"So that was why you were fiddling with the wires."

"I wasn't fiddling! But it didn't matter. The only way to fix the problem was to restart the camera, but there was no point in doing so, seeing as we only had a few minutes left in the taping."

"Is that why you pulled off his headphones and made that sign for cutting someone's throat?"

"You saw that? Yes, but I didn't mean that I was going to kill him. I meant for him to cut the power and step aside, which he did. The camera was down; there was no reason for him to stand there behind a defunct camera."

"So you told him to go backstage?"

"I didn't tell him anything. We were recording, which is why we used hand gestures. I assume he understood me and followed me backstage. Once we were behind the curtain, I didn't pay attention to his movements."

"That makes sense." I tried to shoot around him, but he caught my elbow instead. The jerking motion caused my jacket to shift, and I feared it was going to slide off the box. Yet, before it could, Cindy's assistant rushed into the hallway. "Anton—the police want to speak with you again."

"What now? I already answered their questions," he grumbled.

When Theresa glanced over me, her eyes widened slightly as her eyes crossed over my torso, but she said nothing. Was the box that obvious, I wondered, feeling like an amateur.

The director looked down to my jacket once more before locking eyes with me. "We aren't finished talking. I'll find you later."

Before I could respond to his threat, he turned on his heel and caught up to Theresa, already halfway to the podium.

13

Bad Seeds

When I returned to the others, there was a flurry of activity and a buzz of excitement circling the room. Before I could ask what was going on, Rhonda looked up at me expectantly. "Did you get it?"

"Yes, I did." I dropped to one knee and deposited the box and my jacket on top of her gigantic tote bag. Luckily, Rhonda hadn't filled it to the brim, making it easier to shove the box under her emergency makeup set and hairbrush.

Rhonda bit her lip. "I still don't think we should take it out of the church. What if the police decide they need to examine it further?"

I blew out my cheeks. "They've already dusted it for prints, but left it behind, which tells me they don't consider it of use or importance."

"Maybe not now, but—"

"Rhonda, the officer who interviewed me made it quite clear that the local police are not interested in the box or any treasure it may lead to; all they care about is finding Jan's murderer. It's not my fault they can't see that the two may be connected. Now, can one of you tell me what is going on? The room is abuzz with some sort of news, I can feel it."

"It looks like the police did take your information seriously. They've just pulled one of the audience members aside and are questioning him."

"It must be one of the bad seeds' relatives!" I exclaimed. "We have to figure out what they are saying. Maybe Joris can translate for us."

Myrtle sprung up. "Great thinking. Let's go ask him."

Joris was already standing quite close to the group of officers surrounding a middle-aged man with slicked-back hair and a fancy suit. When I asked for his assistance, he was eager to oblige. *We sure did luck out with him*, I thought.

He kept his eyes on the suspect. "Let me listen, then I'll translate everything for you, okay?"

I nodded and took a step back, to wait with Myrtle. When the police took a moment to confer, Joris caught us up. "The police found the bad seeds' names in the letters and they discovered that someone in the audience has the same last name as one of them—this man, Rene Vlught."

Joris nodded at him. "He's the guy I saw sneaking along the podium towards the end of the taping."

"Oh my!" Rhonda exclaimed.

"Okay, what have the police learned so far?" I asked.

"He's the owner of a successful gallery in Amsterdam. He says that his grandfather told him about Jan's granddad and how he'd stolen away a crate of artwork from the Klavers resistance group during the war. One he claims has not yet been recovered."

My eyebrow arched. "Oh, really? So he's implying that Jan's grandfather is the profiteer who had stolen the art for his own gains?"

"That's correct. But Rene claims to have only come to the taping because he was curious to see what was inside the box. He swears he wouldn't have killed Jan for that scarf. So far, they haven't found it on his person, which isn't helping them build a case against him."

I started to speak, but Joris held up a finger. The police were questioning Rene again, and the cameraman wanted to hear the answer. Whatever they were discussing was making the gallery owner more agitated by the second.

"What is Rene getting so worked up about?" I finally whispered, unable to wait for another pause.

"He's saying that his granddad told him how the Klavers used coded messages to transmit the locations of the underground bunkers. There were rumors that after the war, the survivors were given puzzle boxes made by the grandfather, and that they contained the location of the person's belongings.

Rene had never believed his grandfather's stories, until he saw that puzzle box on television and recognized the Klavers name. That's why he's here."

"Wait, are you saying Rene's grandfather believed that Jan's grandfather left behind a coded message in a puzzle box, one that leads to the missing art's location?"

Joris nodded. "That's what it sounds like."

"Well, what do you think? Were coded messages common in the Second World War?"

"Yes, they were." Joris scratched at the stubble on his chin. "Most resistance groups used codes of one sort or another to pass intel or orders on. There were hundreds of different ways to encode something, and the only requirement was that the receiver would know how to decipher it."

"Okay, that means it must the code can't be too difficult."

"Not necessarily. It could have been quite complex, but as long as the key to deciphering it was known to both, it wouldn't have mattered."

"That scarf must be some kind of decoy. There must be another clue hidden somewhere in that box," I mumbled, glad I had already taken it. Yet in light of this new information, the police may want to take the box into evidence after all. We would have to examine it straight away, so we could return it, if need be. After all, I wanted to help the police with their investigation, not hinder it.

Joris's eyes widened slightly at my mumblings, but he didn't respond to them. Instead, he stepped forward again to better hear Rene's answers. The longer the police questioned the bad seed's descendant, the more hysterical he became. I tapped my foot in frustration as I waited for Rene to stop talking so that Joris could translate everything.

When the cameraman finally stepped back to join us, his expression was quite somber. "The police don't believe Rene was only here to watch, but they don't believe his story about there being a coded message in the box, either. One officer even called it silly."

Relief flowed through me. That meant they wouldn't be searching for the puzzle box anytime soon, so Myrtle, Rhonda, and I could continue on without having to worry about hindering their investigation.

I still had trouble believing that the police were ruling the possibility out, especially since it appeared that someone had believed in the story about the hidden art, enough to kill him for what had been found inside of the box. Whether it was Rene Vlught, I could not say. But it was now clear that this story about Jan's granddad and the missing artwork was well-known, at least in certain circles. Which meant there may be more people searching for it.

I was dying to tear that box apart in our search for another clue. Yet, until we could get away from the police, I didn't dare examine it.

Rene's rising voice made us all turn to look, just in time to see two officers escorting him outside.

Joris listened for a moment to Rene's protests, before a grin spread over his face. "Well, well, the police are taking him in for an official interview and he's yelling for his lawyer."

"That's great, and really fast!" Rhonda exclaimed.

"Indeed," I muttered as another thought brought a smile to my lips. If they had a suspect in custody, the chance that we would soon be free to go had just increased exponentially.

14

Checking In With Rhonda

Apparently I was not the only one who expected our release to be imminent. Before we could pump Joris for more information, Cindy clapped her hands together. "Excuse me, can I have the crew assemble by the podium. Thank you."

Her shrill voice echoed around the space, sending several stagehands and crew members beelining towards the other side of the church.

Joris looked to the stage. "I should join them."

I held out my hand. "Thanks for all of your help. We really appreciate it."

"Sure thing. If you find any more documents you need translating, give me a ring." He shook my hand and inclined his head at Myrtle and Rhonda, before joining the crew.

Rhonda looked up at me expectantly. "So, what do you suggest we do now?"

"Examine the box for another clue, of course. The scarf must have been a decoy. But we can't do it here. So we need to wait until we get back to the hotel to check it for more openings, I'm afraid."

Myrtle nodded towards the other side of the church, where the interviews were taking place. "Hopefully we won't be here much longer. It looks like the police are removing tables, so they must be done with the interviews."

I followed her sightline and took in the scene before nodding in agreement. The majority of the audience members were now milling around their side of the church, and no longer waiting in the pews.

"As soon as they release us, let's head back to the hotel and examine this."

"Sounds good, as long as we order up some sandwiches and a pot of strong coffee, first. We've been cooped up here for hours, and no one's thought to bring us any food or drinks. I'm starving," Rhonda grumbled.

I checked my watch, surprised to see that it was already two in the afternoon. Meaning we'd been in this church since nine in the morning, an hour before the taping began.

"How's your knee? Are you able to walk back to the hotel, do you think? Or do we need to order a cab? I don't want you to end up in a wheelchair, like my partner. We might need to do some serious walking tomorrow, depending on what we learn tonight."

Rhonda pooh-poohed my remark away. "The wound is deep, but it feels like that paramedic got all of the glass out. After a good night's rest, I'll be good to go. Our hotel's beds are super comfy so sleep won't be a problem. But before we investigate anything, I want to call Julie and let her know what's going on. I would hate for her to find out about this incident via the media, instead of me. She might be worried, if she sees this on television later."

"Great point. We wouldn't want to worry her for no reason. And there's no real rush to decode the mystery, as far as I'm concerned. It's been hidden away for decades; a few more hours won't matter," I reasoned.

Before either Myrtle or Rhonda could respond, my bestie's phone beeped, alerting her to a new message. Her face broke out into a wide grin as she gazed at the screen. "Speak of the devil! It's Julie, and she's already at the hotel. Thanks, Carmen. That was really thoughtful of you."

I cocked my head at Rhonda. "That's great that she's here, but why thank me?"

Rhonda pointed her phone's screen at me. "Because Julie said you were the one who contacted her."

I rolled my eyes and slapped my forehead with an open palm. "Sorry, yes, I did text her while I was waiting to talk to the police. I guess with everything going on, I forgot to mention it. Gosh, I didn't expect her to fly over so quickly, but it's great that she did."

"That's alright. I'm just glad you did."

I smiled sweetly, wondering how Julie had really found out about the events that had transpired during the taping of *Antiques Time*. It sounded like I wouldn't have to wait much longer to find out.

15

Julie Shares A Secret

By the time we got back to the hotel, we were all exhausted.

"Shall we examine the box in my room, or one of yours?" I asked Myrtle and Rhonda as our taxi pulled up to the hotel's entrance.

"Your room is fine by me," my bestie replied.

"Sounds good. I'm on the third floor." Since we had all checked in at different moments, our rooms were spread apart, instead of next to each other. I didn't care either way, as the hotel was small enough that the other rooms were easy to reach.

As much as I wanted to rip Rhonda's bag open and examine that puzzle box straight away, I knew I needed to refuel my body first, otherwise I'd probably fall asleep before we got very far. But first, I had a goddaughter to interrogate. However, I figured her mother would want a few minutes alone with her before she'd be willing to share her offspring with me.

As soon as we entered the lobby, a familiar voice rang out. "Mom! Thank goodness you're okay!"

Rhonda's head jerked in her daughter's direction before she threw open her arms and ran towards her. "Julie, darling! I'm so glad you're here!"

When they embraced, I noted that Rhonda's eyes were already glistening. She half turned to Myrtle, all the while keeping her arm firmly around her child's waist, as she proudly introduced her to my company contact.

"Myrtle, this is my baby girl, Julie."

Julie blushed as she held out her hand. "Nice to meet you."

However, once the niceties had concluded, Rhonda ignored us and focused on reassuring her child that she was perfectly fine, despite the bandaged knee.

Myrtle patted my arm. "That was sure thoughtful of you to call Julie, Carmen. I can already tell that Rhonda is relieved to have her here."

I bit my tongue, dying to get Julie alone so I could get the full story. I looked over at mother and daughter, my curiosity piqued as to how my goddaughter really found out about Jan's death during Rhonda's show. But when I saw them holding hands and chatting softly with their foreheads touching, I figured my interrogation could wait.

"We should leave them alone so they can catch up," I whispered to Myrtle. "That Interpol agent hasn't gotten in touch with me yet. What about you?"

"No, nothing," Myrtle confirmed.

"Let me call her and see where she's at. She'll want to see the box, I bet."

Julie must have heard our conversation despite our soft tones, for she broke free from her mother's grasp and jerked her head up at me. "Mom, do you mind if I have a quick word with Aunt Carmen?"

Before Rhonda could reply, Julie had already turned to Myrtle. "Could you help Mom up to her room? Lying on the bed would be better for her knee, I think. We'll be right up."

"Sure thing. Let's get you upstairs." Myrtle grabbed Rhonda's arm and led her towards the elevator before Julie could get a kiss in.

"I'm not an invalid, Myrtle! Thanks for coming over so quickly, Julie. I feel better just having you here."

Once Myrtle and Rhonda were in the lift and going up, Julie turned to me. "Did Myrtle give you the Interpol agent's telephone number?"

"She did." I cocked my head at her. "But how did you know that an agent had been sent over?"

"It's a long story. Why don't you give her a call first, then we'll talk."

I did as asked and waited for the line to connect. A second later, Julie's phone began to ring. "Oh, excuse me. I better take this." When she stepped aside to answer it, I heard in my ear, "Hey, Aunt Carmen. I think I have some explaining to do."

"Julie, why do you have that Interpol agent's phone?"

Her laugh filled the open line. "I thought you, of all people, would understand, Aunt Carmen. You know that new job I mentioned? It's for Interpol. I'm Dave Swanson's partner. Well, technically he's my mentor. I'm still in training."

When Julie's words sunk in, I swear you could have knocked me over with a feather. "Seriously? You are the agent Dave's boss sent over? You work for Interpol, too?"

Julie hung up and crossed back over to face me. There was a steely determination in her expression, one that I had never seen in her before. "Surprise?"

I leaned my head against the wall and closed my eyes. Julie being an Interpol agent and Dave's partner explained so much about her odd behavior these past few weeks. "So you aren't based out of Prague anymore, are you?"

"No, I'm not. Dave and I have offices at Interpol's headquarters in Lyon, France. But I'm off on assignment so much, I'm not there often."

"Were you at that auction in Luxembourg? I swore I saw someone who looked like you leaving when we arrived."

'Yep, that was me. I was so shocked to see Mom walk in the door and you trailing behind. I knew that you were an agent for Rosewood, but we didn't know you would be attending the same auction."

"Some agent I am. I had no idea you and Dave were partners. I actually thought you two might have dated, based on your strangely aloof reaction when you met him supposedly for the first time in Venice."

Julie pulled a face as if she'd bitten into a lemon. "As if, he's almost old enough to be my dad! I think our cover as a couple only works so well because most of the older men we target have young trophy wives on their arms."

I was shocked to realize how pleased it made me to learn that she and Dave had never been romantically involved and that the discomfort I had sensed was because they were hiding the fact that they worked together.

"Your mother is going to kill you when she finds out you're doing something so dangerous!" I blurted out.

Julie threw her hands on her hips. "You're one to talk. Does Mom know you work as an art sleuth for the Rosewood Agency, Aunt Carmen?"

I gritted my jaw. "Touché, young lady. No, she does not. How long have you known?"

"Since Dave told me about how you'd upset the French police by insisting the Rosewood Agency be allowed to return Harold Moreau's Book of Hours to the American museum it had been stolen from."

"That was almost two months ago. You've known all this time?"

My goddaughter suppressed a giggle. "Honestly, I didn't believe Dave when he told me the name of the agent. All of these years you've been working as an art recovery specialist, and none of us knew. I actually showed him pictures of you, just to make certain we were talking about the same Carmen De Luca. So you managed to keep Mom in the dark this entire time. She really doesn't know why you are here in Europe?"

I shook my head. "She thinks I'm a reporter for an antiques magazine, one with really cushy assignments."

"You've worked for Rosewood for more than fifteen years! Geez, I knew Mom was gullible, but I would have expected her to have picked up a few clues over the years."

"Look, she's a trusting lady who had no reason to doubt what I told her," I replied, in defense of my friend. In actuality, Rhonda had long assumed I was lying about what I really did for a living, and occasionally tried to call my bluff, but I had remained steadfast in my assertations that I was a journalist and nothing more. Seeing as I had kept to my cover story for the past fifteen years, telling her the truth now, after all this time deceiving her, was not something I relished having to do. Frankly, I was terrified that her learning the truth about my job would destroy our friendship.

Apparently Julie interrupted my hesitation as a crisis of conscience. "I guess we both have secrets we are keeping from her. Or are you planning on exposing me to Mom?"

"It depends. What exactly are you doing these days?"

"I'm assigned to the same division as Dave, as a junior agent-in-training.

So far, it's been quite challenging, but rewarding."

"And dangerous," I hissed.

"I don't know, my work is quite similar to that of an art recovery specialist, like yourself."

I studied her carefully. On the one hand, her work was risky and full of potentially deadly situations. I could understand why Rhonda would be worried, if she knew the true nature of her job. On the other hand, Julie was a thoughtful and intelligent adult who was quite capable of taking care of herself, it seemed. Who was I to tattle on her to her mother? "No, I won't say anything, at least, as long as you keep quiet about the Rosewood Agency."

Julie stuck out her hand. "It's a deal."

After I accepted, she added, "Now, shall we talk to Myrtle about how we're going to figure out who killed that kid and why? I know she's your company contact at the Rosewood Agency. Reggie speaks highly of her."

I narrowed my eyes at her, realizing I was going to have to be wary about what I said around her from now on. "He would; it is his mother, after all. But you already knew that, didn't you?"

Julie unsuccessfully tried to repress a smile.

"If Myrtle does not yet know you are with Interpol, then I suggest that we do not enlighten her, at least not yet."

"Why?"

"Because if you tell Myrtle who you work for now, she may slip up and say something about it in front of Rhonda. I think you should tell your mom first—you owe her that much."

Julie considered my words. "You make a great point, but I'm not ready to tell Mom. Do you promise to keep me updated?"

I crossed my fingers behind my back before answering. "I certainly will. Now, let's head up to Rhonda's room and see if we can figure out if there is anything in that puzzle box!"

16

Wartime Grannies

As we ascended the stairs, I caught Julie up on all that had happened during and after the show's taping. She listened without comment, only nodding to signal that she'd heard me.

By the time we reached the hotel room, I had high hopes that Rhonda and Myrtle had already figured out how to open the box. After all, Rhonda had spent hours researching all the ways to get into it.

Yet neither had gotten very far. In fact, Rhonda was softly snoring when Myrtle let us into the room.

My company contact shrugged. "She nodded off a few minutes ago and looked so peaceful I didn't want to disturb her."

"We need her help with the box. She's already spent hours looking up all the possible combinations, and that would save us so much time." I ticked my tongue against my teeth, yet after another glance at her angelic expression, I understood Myrtle's decision. "Oh, what the heck. I suppose we can examine it later."

Julie looked at me as if I was crazy. "After everything that's happened because of this box, you're willing to wait a few more hours to try to open it? No way. It's time to get cracking."

She grabbed ahold of her mother's foot and gently shook it. "Mom, you're snoring. We need your expertise—can you wake up?"

Rhonda's eyes blinked open at her daughter's voice. She slowly sat up, then wiped the drool from one corner of her mouth. "Gosh, sorry about that. I must have dozed off."

She swung her legs over the edge of the bed. "Okay, shall we see why this box is so important?"

I rubbed my hands together. "Yes, ma'am."

Julie stood up and crossed over to the nightstand. "While you three are doing that, I'm going to do a little research into the Klavers resistance group and see if I can find out more about them. That may help illuminate this situation. But first, let's order some room service."

"Now you're talking, kiddo. I would love a turkey club."

Rhonda raised a finger. "Make that two."

"I would kill for a BLT, if they have one on the menu," Myrtle said.

"Got it." Julie picked up the hotel phone to order as my bestie pulled the puzzle box out of her tote bag.

I eyed the object on her lap. "If there's another secret compartment in that thing, we should be able to find it. What do you think, Rhonda—could there be another opening?"

"I suppose so. Once I found the scarf, I stopped looking. But from my research online, there are only a handful of ways that most of these boxes worked. It's just a matter of trying them all until we find one that works."

She pushed on several of the inlaid strips of wood, and jiggled it close to her ear as she did. It took her about a half hour to test the combinations she could recall, but none produced the desired effect.

"Why don't we search online again for other possibilities?" Julie suggested.

I grabbed the box and studied its inlaid surface. "Before we do, could you open up the first secret space again, Rhonda?"

"Sure thing. It's pretty simple, once you know the code."

After she had gotten it open, I fiddled with the panels inside the hidden space, prodding them as I tested my theory. I reckoned if the scarf was a decoy, the second compartment may very well be accessible via the first.

When I pushed on the center of the back wall rather firmly, one of the inlaid strips on the outside left of the box sprung open. I grinned up at the others as I pulled it further out, revealing a tiny drawer. Resting on the velvet-lined interior was a large, old-fashioned-looking key about as long as my ring finger.

Myrtle whistled under her breath just as Rhonda exclaimed, "That must be what the thief was after!"

Julie put a hand on my shoulder and squeezed. "Well done, Aunt Carmen."

I blushed at her compliment. "Without your mother's help, I never would have found it."

I picked the key up, feeling its weight as I turned it over in my hand. The handle was shaped into a flat cloverleaf that seemed to have been created from the same piece of metal that formed the long shank ending in a thick key.

"The slot this fit into must also be quite large and deep. Unfortunately, I don't see any markings on it that make clear what kind of lock this is meant to open. But I bet we're going to need this later."

Rhonda closed my fingers over the key. "I think you're right. You should hang onto it, Carmen."

I pocketed it, then stared down at the box. "Okay, so we found an old key, which makes me feel like this is the puzzle box Jan's granddad was referring to in his last letter. But we haven't found anything that looks like a code. I don't see any letters or numbers scratched into the surface. Do any of you?"

"No, but I haven't really taken a good look at it." Myrtle grabbed the box off the bed and proceeded to inspect every inch of it. Her frown told me what I needed to know.

"Julie, do you want to take a look?"

"What's the point—you three have examined it and found nothing. Maybe Jan's dad had removed whatever was encoded. For all we know, he'd already searched for the art but didn't find it."

"I'm afraid Julie is right," her mother chimed in. "Until we figure out where the code is, we are stuck."

We all stared down at the box, lost in silence, until Rhonda asked, "What should we do with this? The police may want to examine it, after they've interviewed Rene Vlught. I would prefer not to hinder an official investigation."

Myrtle tapped her chin. "Maybe you should take the box back to the set today and slip it into the dressing room. The police don't need to know about the key just yet, at least not until we've had a chance to search for another clue. They weren't exactly jumping at the chance to look for the supposedly missing artwork."

Rhonda frowned at Myrtle's suggestion. "The set is closed until the health and safety folks have had a chance to check the electricity. Cindy will call me once she knows when we're going to be able to film again."

I picked the box up again. "Either way, I'm reluctant to return it just yet. What if this box has more secrets to share? We still don't know where to look next, or even if Jan's granddad really did leave an encoded message behind. I mean, all we've found is a key and tacky scarf. Which means we've missed something, or this is not the box Jan's granddad was referring to. Maybe there's a slip of paper that got lodged in between the drawer and lid." I started to shake the box as hard as I could, when Julie's chortle stopped me short.

"You have got to be kidding me!"

"What is there?" her mother cried.

"Hey gals, we may have already found the code." My goddaughter grinned up at us as she held her phone's screen towards us. "Check this out. I just Googled 'WWII' and 'knitted scarf,' and guess what I found. Have you heard of steganography?"

"Isn't that the art of hiding secret messages in plain sight?" I offered.

"Yep, and there's a whole article about it on *Atlas Obscura*. It seems that little old ladies made great spies during World War II. Apparently Dutch grannies often helped the resistance by knitting coded messages into scarves and sweaters that could be easily passed along without raising suspicion." Julie's grin lit up the room. "Maybe the scarf contains a coded message!"

Myrtle slapped a hand against her forehead. "Of course! Why didn't I think of that earlier? Steganography has been used effectively for thousands of years because it is easy to overlook. The code could be worked into a pattern—or made to look like a mistake in the stitching."

I leaned back into the sofa and groaned. "That's great work, Julie, but unfortunately a moot point, at least until the police manage to find the scarf.

I doubt the closeups of it from the television will be clear enough to figure out what message was encoded in it."

"Would photos suffice?"

We all turned to Rhonda, whose face was split with a grin.

I cocked my head at her. "What are you talking about?"

Rhonda held her phone up so we could see the screen. "Tada!"

It was a closeup of the top portion of the scarf. "How the heck did you get pictures of it?" I asked, incredulous.

"Sweetie, did you really think I would try to figure out how to open up a decades-old puzzle box, live on air?"

I stared at her incredulously. In fact, that was what I thought had happened. "Yes?"

Rhonda grinned at me before slapping a hand on the tip of her good knee, guffawing as she added, "I can't believe it—I fooled the great Carmen De Luca! I opened the box the night of the first taping, thus before I opened it live on air."

"But why?"

Rhonda snorted. "I can't be fumbling around on live television—Cindy would never allow it. So I looked up the combinations most commonly used by puzzle makers in that period and worked it out eventually. They aren't as unique as you'd think. Finding that scarf was a real letdown, but I figured if Jan's grandfather hid it away like that, it must be important, somehow. That's why I took so many pictures of it. After that, I put it back just as I'd found it, and acted surprised when Jan pulled the scarf out of the drawer, live on television."

"Well, I'll be…" I leaned back, flabbergasted at having been fooled by my bestie.

Rhonda's grin spread from cheek to cheek. "I'm a pretty good actress, aren't I? Maybe I should work with you on a few more undercover articles, after all."

17

Solving Another Puzzle

Our sandwiches arrived soon after Julie called our order in, and we gladly took a break to indulge in our first real meal of the day. Thanks to the discovery of the key and the article in *Atlas Obscura*, we were all feeling pretty good about ourselves and this treasure hunt and complimented each other's insights between bites.

After we were all sated, Rhonda held her phone out to Myrtle. "Here you go. You'd mentioned earlier how much you love to knit. Maybe you can make some sense of this."

I leaned forward and clasped my hands together. "What can you tell us about the knitting? Could it be a coded pattern, or has the knitter spelled out letters in the scarf?"

"Give me a chance to examine the thing, Carmen," Myrtle grumbled.

I held up my palms. "Right, sorry. I'll back off."

My company contact held the photos close to her eye and studied them intently before declaring, "This is by far the worst knitting I have ever seen. At least, at first glance. However, on closer inspection, it looks like the knitter created a pattern of lines and balls in the middle that could be a code."

Myrtle turned the phone so Rhonda and I could see the photo better, then pointed to one section of it. "See here? These lines are pulled too long, and the knitter made little balls out of the wool far too often to match the rest of the design. If we weren't expecting to find a coded message in this thing, I would have said that it was a mistake made by a tired knitter. Especially since the next part is quite consistent. I bet this is the section we are interested in."

From Myrtle's smug expression, it was clear that she was confident in her assessment. I knew she was an avid knitter, and a pretty good one, at that. During my early years with the company, Myrtle had given every employee a hand-knitted scarf one Christmas, and I had been surprised at how well-made it was. I still had it and wore it often.

"Alright. Let's all take a turn examining that section closely." After the phone had done a round robin, I looked to the other three. "So, what do we see, ladies?"

"All I see are stripes and balls," Julie ventured.

"Stripes and balls…" Myrtle repeated softly until her voice trailed off completely and her eyelids fluttered closed. Suddenly, her eyes shot open. "Wait a second—could it be that simple?"

She grabbed Rhonda's phone out of my hand and brought the image close to her eye. "Well, I'll be. If those stripes are meant to be dashes, and the balls are dots, then this could be Morse code. It is binary, after all. I used to be able to read it, but it's been a while."

"I can read Morse code," Rhonda piped up.

I regarded my bestie. "I didn't know that."

Rhonda giggled. "It's not something I do often. My dad had served in the Navy and taught me to read it when I was a kid. We practiced so often, I still remember most of the letters."

Myrtle handed Rhonda one of the closeups, and she began to read through the message letter for letter.

"Let's see… V…I…N…D are the first four letters. Then this stripe indicates a space." Rhonda stopped and stared at the photo. "Maybe I don't recall it as well as I thought. This is gibberish."

"What do you mean?" I asked.

"My memory tells me this first word is 'vind.' That's no English word I've ever heard of."

"Maybe it's an old-fashioned term? Or code for something?" Myrtle suggested.

I typed "vind" into my phone's browser, and the search engine automatically recognized it as a Dutch word and translated it into English for me. Sometimes I really loved technology.

"Or the message is in Dutch," I laughed. "Which would make sense, considering a Dutch person probably knitted it. According to Google Translate, 'vind' means 'find.' Can you keep decoding it, letter for letter?"

"Great! After 'vind' and space, it reads…"

I transcribed the letters as Rhonda slowly read them off one by one, before typing it all into my phone and translating the text in its entirety. "*Vind Westerstraete ter Hazelbroek. Vijftien vuisten onder de aardbol van Atlas.*"

I stared at the screen a moment. "Well, it is most definitely Dutch. But it's a little cryptic. The message translates as: 'Find Westerstraete in Hazelbroek. Fifteen fists under Atlas's globe.'"

Rhonda's eyebrows knitted together. "You're right, that is cryptic."

"Okay, so are Hazelbroek and Westerstraete places or people? And what could that reference to Atlas mean? Maybe the whole thing is in code and means something completely different," I argued.

Julie was already back on her phone. "We're in luck. Hazelbroek is a small village in the south close to the border with Belgium. The grandfather's letters did suggest that his resistance group were moving artwork down south, which would suggest that Hazelbroek is not in code, but a reference to a real village."

She began to read aloud the results she was finding about the village, located in the Ardennes, a region in the south of the Netherlands fairly close to the German and Belgian borders. The more we learned, the more it felt as if the artwork being in Hazelbroek wasn't far-fetched at all. It had been an active battlefield during the Second World War, and there were lots of underground bunkers and hiding places in the hilly, wooded area surrounding most of the villages.

The village was also situated quite close to Overloon, where an impressive-looking military museum was located. From the website, it appeared that parts of the exhibition were set up inside underground bunkers that had been built during the war. If we came up short, perhaps one of their volunteers would be able to help us further. Or Joris, I realized, recalling that I still had his number in my phone. He was quite knowledgeable about the war and resistance groups.

That thought gave me pause. He did claim to be a WWII buff, but he didn't know about steganography or the possibility that the scarf could have been encoded. My eyes narrowed as my thoughts darkened. But when I shared them with Rhonda, she pooh-pooh'ed my remark away. "Joris was a big help to us. I don't know why you have to say those mean things about him."

I blew out my cheeks, not in the mood to get into an argument over this.

Luckily Julie intervened. "Listen to this—according to my search results, Westerstraete appears to be a fairly common name for people, places, and streets in the Netherlands. If it is a person, they may know where the art is, though I do wonder if they'll still be alive. It was so long ago. Or it might be the location where we'll find Atlas and his globe."

"Westerstraete sounds like a last name to me," Myrtle offered. "I think we should focus on finding any families named Westerstraete who live in Hazelbroek. I don't get the Atlas clue, but maybe when we find this Westerstraete, he can explain it, or more likely his relatives. Julie's right, the chance of them still being alive is pretty slim. I only hope he passed his secret along."

"I agree that we should follow this lead," Rhonda said, seconding the idea.

"Then it's settled," Julie added. "We need to drive down there and take a look around. Don't you agree, Aunt Carmen?"

I nodded, glad my goddaughter had a solid head on her shoulders.

Rhonda covered a yawn with her hand. "What do you say we ask the hotel's receptionist to rent us a car? I can use the show's credit card. It's already six o'clock and I'm so beat, I don't feel up to driving down tonight. We could leave first thing in the morning. After a good night's sleep, I know I'll be able to think more clearly."

I wrapped an arm around her shoulder. "I think that's a great idea. After we get our transportation sorted, why don't we grab some dinner in the hotel restaurant? That sandwich wasn't enough to stop my stomach from rumbling."

18

Another Break-In

When we returned to our rooms, practically rolling down the hallway because we'd stuffed ourselves silly on the scrumptious Indonesian buffet in the hotel's restaurant, all I wanted to do was soak in the bath until my eyelids drooped close. However, seeing my hotel door cracked open put a kibosh on that plan.

When I pushed on the door with my foot, it swung open to reveal a ransacked space. My blouses, skirts, trousers, underwear, and pantyhose were strewn across the furniture and bed. The floor was littered with my shoe collection and bags. On the back of one chair hung my favorite pantsuit, a large tear visible in one of the legs.

"Dang it! What is the meaning of this?" I yelped, angry that someone had manhandled my belongings.

My ranting caused Myrtle, Rhonda, and Julie to tear back out to the hallway. I pointed inside my open door. "Somebody broke into my room during dinner!"

Rhonda's hands flew to her face. "Oh no!"

Myrtle peeked around me. "But who would do such a thing? And what do you think they were after?"

From the doorway, I studied my belongings. There was something off about the scene before me that my brain wanted me to notice, but it wasn't registering. "I do not know. It's like they set a bomb off inside of my suitcase.

With everything strewn around, it's going to take a while to figure that out. But I don't want to go inside until the police have dusted for fingerprints."

"How the heck did they get in?" Rhonda asked.

I bent down to examine the slot. "These locks aren't that sturdy. You can get them open with a credit card and a forceful hip bump."

Rhonda's eyebrows shot up. "Why do you know that?"

I ignored her question and looked inside the room again. Why was my brain niggling me to look closer? My eyes swept over the sight before me, and this time I tried to ignore my clothing and see the rest of the scene. Seconds later, it clicked. "Oh, nuts—the box is missing! I'd left it on that table next to the bed."

I'd brought it with me when I'd popped back into my room to change clothes before dinner. Part of me wondered whether there was a third compartment that we had not yet found, and part of me just enjoyed gazing upon such a gorgeously handcrafted piece.

"We need to check the room for it!" Rhonda took one step inside, but my arm held her back.

"Let's call the cops, first. The perpetrator may have left behind a fingerprint or two. They should also be able to get access to the camera footage of the hallway." I pointed to a glass eye mounted onto the hallway's ceiling.

"Carmen's right. We shouldn't enter until they've processed the room. We can call them from mine," Myrtle added.

While we waited for the cops to show up, I struggled to grasp how the thief had known to find the box in my room. It seemed that I wasn't the only one wondering, too. "Who would have known that Carmen had the box and why would someone want to steal it?" Myrtle mused aloud.

"If they believed Rene's story about it containing a clue to the whereabouts of a cache of missing art, then pretty much anyone in the church would have had a motive for taking it. But that doesn't help us figure out who saw me take it," I groused. It didn't help that I hadn't been subtle enough when I'd lifted the box from the dressing room—that was apparent from the way the director stared at me. But he'd not tattled on me to the police. Why? Had he hoped to steal it from me, later? And if Anton had seen me take it, who else had noticed?

Before I could beat myself up for being so careless, Myrtle's phone rang. Her expression brightened as she listened to the caller. When she hung up, she announced with a grin, "The cops are here. A porter is escorting them up to your room now."

After two officers entered the hallway, I couldn't honestly answer their most pressing question—why someone would have broken in. If I told them the truth, that I had taken Jan's box from the dressing room without asking permission first, I would have to also explain why I had done so. Right now, I was not willing to share my theories with these policemen. The ones I had already shared them with didn't believe a word of it. Why would these cops be any different?

They were almost done questioning us when another uniformed officer joined us. He had a laptop with him and showed us a short video fragment of our burglar entering the room by way of credit card and hip bump—just as I'd suspected. But the person was wearing a bulky jacket, scarf, and hat that shielded their identity. At first I presumed they were male, but after a second viewing, I realized it could have been a woman with lots of layers on. When the person opened the door, there was a brief flash of white emanating from their wrist.

"Wait a second—did you see that flash? Would it be a watch or bracelet?"

The officer backed the footage up so we could all watch it again.

"It does look like the light caught on the thief's watch face and reflected it back. The spotlights in the hallway are quite bright," the officer concluded.

"If it is a unique piece, Rhonda or I may recognize it and then we can try to track down the owner," I said, my excitement causing my words to rush out.

"Could you play it once more?"

When he did as requested, I concentrated all of my attention on that burst of light, trying to get a glimpse of that watch, but it happened too fast. I slouched down in my chair. "Shoot, I can't tell what it is, or even if it is a watch."

"That's alright. What can you tell us about the person? There were too many guests moving through the lobby for this person to have stood out.

Are you all certain that you do not recognize them?"

"I can't even tell if that's a man or woman!" Myrtle exclaimed.

I shook my head. "I'm sorry, but without seeing the person's face, we can't help you."

The lead officer nodded to the cop with the laptop, who then closed the computer down.

He looked us all over once more, as if he was unsure as to how to proceed. "Alright. You are free to pack up your belongings. The receptionist has arranged for another room for you, Miss De Luca. Here is your key."

I nodded my thanks as I took the hotel key from his outstretched hand.

The lead detective cleared his throat, garnering our attention once again. "We will be in touch as soon as we know more. I bid you a good night." He bowed ever so slightly before he and his men retreated to the lobby.

Once the officers had left, Rhonda patted my arm. "Let's get packed up and move you into your new room."

I squeezed her hand. "It's okay, you don't have to help me. Why don't you take a bath, instead? You deserve a little R&R."

"Are you certain?"

"Very much so."

"I bet those cops are going to figure out who broke into your room," Rhonda announced as she stood before her door.

"That's true, it is best to keep thinking positive." I smiled, but internally I felt like frowning. The officer's words held little promise that he would find the culprit anytime soon.

I stretched my arms high over my head, and let my jaw crack with a yawn. "If you ladies don't mind, I'm going to hit the sack. What do you say we meet for breakfast at six? It's a few hours' drive, and that'll give us all day to search for whatever clue Jan's granddad may have left behind."

Rhonda blew a kiss in my direction. "Sounds good. Sleep tight, you hear?"

"Thanks, Rhonda. Good night, you two." Despite my word choice, I doubted the pair would get to sleep anytime soon, but would instead be up all night chatting. Now that they'd reconciled, they had a lot to catch up on, and they were as bad as teenagers when it came to lights out.

Julie pecked both Myrtle and me on the cheek before joining her mom.

Myrtle looked up at me. "Are you sure you want to be alone? You can sleep in my room, if you're feeling vulnerable."

I shook my head, recalling how loudly she snored. At least in my own room, I could sleep soundly. "Thanks for the offer, but I'll be fine on my own. I'll see you in the morning, okay?"

"Sure thing. Sleep well."

19

Updates From Cindy

We were halfway through our breakfast, still a bit groggy thanks to the early hour, when Rhonda's phone rang.

She gulped back a swig of freshly pressed orange juice before answering. "This is Rhonda Rhodes. Good morning, Theresa. What can I do for you?"

My bestie listened a minute before answering. "We're at breakfast now, but we're leaving for Hazelbroek in a few minutes. Why, are we filming today?"

I kicked her under the table. "What are you doing?"

"Give me just a second, Theresa, Carmen has a question." Rhonda glared back at me, but at least she held her hand over the receiver so the caller couldn't hear us. "I'm telling my boss's assistant where I'm going to be, in case they need me for the taping. This is my job, after all. What's your problem with her knowing where we are going?"

"I don't know who to trust right now, and even if Cindy and her assistant are on the up-and-up, I don't know if everyone they know is. How does she know where we're going, anyway?"

"Carmen, you are being paranoid. Cindy saw that I'd rented a van with the company credit card and wants to know what my plans are. She messaged me late last night to let me know that Health and Safety would need most of the day to test the equipment, so I can't imagine she's upset that I'm going out of town. But she'll still want to know where her show's star is hanging out. If I was in Cindy's shoes, I would have done the same and had my assistant call to check in."

"Alright. At least don't tell her what we're planning on doing."

"Hello, Rhonda, are you there?" We could hear Theresa yelling through the phone's speaker.

"I'm right here, dear," Rhonda said as she uncovered the receiver. "Sorry about that, Theresa. Do you need me to come to the set?"

The longer she listened, the more concerned she appeared to be.

"Gosh, I can't actually tell how long we'll be gone. I suppose most of the day. But if Cindy would prefer that I stay in town, I will."

Rhonda's relieved expression told me Cindy did not.

"Okay, well, tell Cindy hi for me. I'll see you two tomorrow morning, bright and early. At least, if I don't see you at the hotel later today."

I locked eyes with my friend once she'd hung up. "I don't know how I feel about Theresa and Cindy knowing that we are heading to Hazelbroek. Do you trust them to keep it to themselves?"

Rhonda tapped a finger against her chin. "To be honest, I do not. Neither one of them is a blabbermouth, but if someone asks, they will certainly tell the truth. But if I ask them to keep our destination quiet, that will only raise red flags in both of their minds. I'm afraid we're just going to have to hope that no one asks."

I took in her answer as I considered what I knew about the two women. Cindy was as hard as nails and someone that most people gave a wide berth to. But her young assistant seemed more approachable. "What can you tell me about Theresa?"

"I'm ashamed to say, not much. She seems nice enough, but does tend to keep to herself most of the time. She has come out of her shell a little bit during this trip, but I've been so busy with the set and Cindy that I haven't really paid attention to her. Cindy trusts her implicitly, so there's that."

"Yeah, there's that." I thought back to my chat with the bubbly young woman yesterday. "Theresa does seem to be having a great time here in Europe and was really grateful to Cindy for inviting her to come along."

"That's true. It was easier to hire locals to film the shows than to fly our crew over, which apparently upset some of them. I do recall Cindy mentioning how grateful Theresa was that she was asked to join her because she'd never have been able to fly to Europe otherwise."

"You're right about that. International travel is incredibly expensive these days. Not just the flights, but the hotels, too. Luckily we have employers willing to pay for our tickets," I laughed.

"Oh, speak of the devil. I guess Cindy's not pleased with our plans, after all," Rhonda exclaimed after her phone began to ring again and she noted who was calling. My bestie punched the speaker button, and Cindy's voice filled the room.

"Hey Rhonda, how are you doing this morning? Is your knee better, or does it still hurt to put pressure on it? I've been worried about you," Cindy groused.

"I'm doing well, thank you. A good night's sleep is all I needed. I'm sorry I didn't check in with you earlier. I was planning on doing just that after breakfast, but your assistant Theresa called a minute ago. I assumed she had done so at your request."

"No, she sure didn't. I asked her to come in early this morning, but she's a no-show."

Rhonda's eyebrows creased. "Wait, what? That doesn't make any sense. She just called me from the set because she saw I'd rented a van and wanted to know what I was planning on doing today."

"Why would she call you to ask that? I'd told her that I'd given you the day off, while we sort out the set and electricity."

I grabbed Rhonda's arm. "Cindy, sorry to eavesdrop on your conversation, but can you tell us when you last saw Theresa?"

"Hey, Carmen. Yesterday evening the crew had dinner and a nightcap at the hotel bar together, after the police released us all. She went up to her room around midnight and I haven't seen her since. She's not picking up her phone, either."

My face drained of color as Cindy's words sank in. "It wasn't a watch."

"What did you say, Carmen?" Rhonda asked.

I leaned in close to my bestie's ear and whispered, "It wasn't a watch, it was a bracelet. Rhonda, I need you to hang up right now. Can you tell Cindy that you'll call her back later?"

My bestie nodded and did as I asked. "I'll call you later today to check in, okay? Good luck!"

Before she could press the "end call" button, we heard Cindy yell out. "Wait—there's something else you should know. The police may have more questions for all of us because they just released Rene Vlught from police custody. I've given them your contact information, so they can call you directly, if need be."

"They did?" I asked.

"Yes. Apparently he finally admitted that his grandfather had stolen several transport trucks full of artwork that had been entrusted to the Klavers group, not Jan's grandfather. That's how his granddad started their family's gallery—by selling the art they'd stolen. He even admitted that he knew about the puzzle box's existence and that he had been waiting for it to resurface."

"Oh, man. That's sick. But why did they let him go?"

"Because they reviewed the camera footage and spotted Rene still seated in the audience, seconds before the lights went out. There was no way he could have gotten to that plug and shorted out the electricity in time."

I looked to Rhonda. "That is a bummer."

"It is, and it means that Jan's killer is still out there," Cindy added. "See you tomorrow, Rhonda?"

"Yep, see you tomorrow."

Rhonda hung up and then studied my face. "Cindy's news was not that positive. So why are you looking as pleased as a peacock?"

"Because I think I know who broke into my room. Now all we have to do is confront the suspect."

"No! We have to call the police if you think you know who killed Jan."

"I don't think this person killed Jan, but they did steal the box. Can you trust me on this one?"

Rhonda pursed her lips, but ultimately nodded her consent. "Okay, I trust you."

"Fabulous. Let me call Theresa back."

"But Cindy said she wasn't picking up."

I winked at my friend. "I have a sneaking suspicion she'll take my call."

20

Charm Bracelet

Sure enough, Theresa picked up on the first ring. "Hey, Theresa, we were wondering if you wanted to drive down to Hazelbroek with us. At least, if you have nothing else to do today. It's supposed to be a pretty little village."

"I would love to. Cindy doesn't need me at the set, after all, so I'm free," Theresa gushed.

"Great. Would you mind coming to the hotel? I don't know if I trust Myrtle to drive through downtown Amsterdam to pick you up."

"Sure thing. I'll be right there!"

Theresa hung up before I could respond.

A half hour later, she was pounding on my hotel room door. "Carmen! Oh, good, you didn't leave without me."

I smiled and waved her in. "Of course not! We are all looking forward to talking with you."

It was only after I closed the door that Theresa seemed to notice Myrtle, Rhonda, and Julie standing across from my bed. All three were glaring at her.

Theresa cowered a little and began to slowly back up. "Why are you staring at me?"

I lunged for her wrist and grabbed ahold of her charm bracelet. "Why did you break into my room and steal Jan's puzzle box? Don't deny it, I saw your bracelet on the hotel's security tape."

Her frightened expression immediately turned to defiance. "You didn't have any right to take it, either. I saw you sneak out of the dressing room with that puzzle box and figured you were looking for another clue to the artwork that Jan mentioned."

I could feel myself paling as her words sunk in. How could I have been so obvious?

"Give me a break. You don't really think there's artwork hidden away somewhere, do you?" Rhonda chuckled. "And even if you do, you broke into Carmen's room, knowing she was my friend. How could you do that to her? Cindy treats you like family and I try to…"

Theresa's cackle cut Rhonda off. "Are you kidding me? If that's how she treats her family, it's no wonder she's still single. Cindy is a horrible boss. She's great at pointing out your faults, but she saves all of her compliments for you, Rhonda. And all you care about are the antiques being featured; you don't give a fig about any of your crew. If I could find another position that paid as well, I'd leave your show in a heartbeat."

"But why would you say that I don't care about the crew? I've never been anything but nice to you."

Theresa jutted her chin up in the air. "Rhonda, you found me crying in the green room last year, because my student debts were overwhelming me financially, and you punched me on the shoulder and told me to keep my chin up. Yet a stranger puts on a sob story and you offer to pay for his entire university degree? That really hurt. So I broke into Carmen's room looking for the box. I figure I'm smart enough to puzzle the mystery out, and if I could find whatever Jan's granddad hid away, then I might be able to pay off my student loans and start over again."

I tried to calmly digest her words and not judge her actions. I knew from my childhood days that being in debt could mess with people's minds and make them do crazy things. There was also a significant difference between stealing and murder. Did Theresa have it in her to kill? I really didn't think so.

"Do you have the box with you?"

Theresa nodded and pulled it out of her backpack. "You can have it back, but you can't call the cops on me. You were the ones who took it from the church—not me."

I tilted my head at her, considering her words. "You're right, but I can call Cindy."

Theresa's head dropped, and she stroked her charm bracelet. "Must you? I was so looking forward to seeing more of Europe."

"I think it's for the best," Rhonda answered. "Maybe being the assistant to a producer is not the career for you. Why not try to find something in the tourism industry, now that we're able to travel again?"

Theresa looked up at Rhonda with doe eyes. "But I need this job, at least, until I can find another one. I'll never be able to pay all of my bills, otherwise."

"Maybe we don't have to tell Cindy right away. She is cooperating, and I really don't think she killed Jan," I whispered.

Rhonda's fierce expression softened a smidgen. "Okay. Let me think on what will be the best course of action. But Theresa, you better promise to keep your nose clean from now on. You hear? No more sneaking around or breaking into hotel rooms."

Theresa sprung up and saluted Rhonda. "Yes, ma'am!"

My bestie eyed the assistant. "And the next time you need financial help, ask for it instead of pussyfooting around about it. Okay?"

"Okay."

Rhonda folded her hands over her torso. "Now why don't you skedaddle before I change my mind about talking to Cindy?"

21

Talking Through The Suspects List

As soon as Theresa had fled the room, I turned to the others. "I say we hotfoot it to the van and get out of town. I don't know who else saw me take that box, but I don't want to wait around to find out."

"I agree. The car's key is at the reception desk," Rhonda said, already halfway out of the door.

The minivan the hotel had rented for us was quite spacious. I sat up front with Myrtle, so Rhonda and her daughter could stretch out in the back for the two-hour ride. I stayed quiet until Myrtle got us out of town, knowing she needed her full concentration to avoid hitting the many bicyclists, trams, and buses competing for space on the same precious few feet of asphalt.

As soon as we hit the highway and I noticed Myrtle's knuckles were no longer white, I turned so I was facing all three women.

"So ladies, if Rene didn't kill Jan, who did? I say we write up a suspect list." I pulled my phone out, ready to note the names.

"It sure sounds like a whole bunch of people saw you take that puzzle box, Carmen. That doesn't help us narrow down our list."

Rhonda's comment made me blush, but before I could retort, Myrtle interceded.

"That's a good point, Rhonda. That story about Jan's box leading to the artwork his granddad hid away seems to be one that many WWII buffs know about. We don't know who was sitting in the audience, but it sounds like pretty much anyone who'd been paying attention to your movements would have noticed that you'd taken the box."

My face felt as if it was on fire. "We have to start somewhere—what about Theresa? She did break in to my room and steal the box." I didn't consider her a serious suspect, but I wanted to shift attention away from my mistake.

Rhonda gasped as my words sunk in. "I understand why she broke into your room, but you don't seriously think her money woes would have caused her to kill Jan, do you?"

"Her debt may give her a reason to be interested in whatever the box would lead to, but it doesn't necessarily mean she had murderous intentions," Julie added.

"I honestly do not know. If she is so worried about her finances, she may have thought that whatever the granddad hid away was worth killing for," I countered.

Myrtle tapped the steering wheel with her thumbs. "I don't know, Carmen. That seems highly unlikely, and I'm usually pretty cynical about this kind of thing. If you want to put her on your list, so be it. But she's not a prime suspect, in my book, anyway."

"Okay, then who do you think did do it and why?" I shot back.

"That director Anton seems like the kind of guy who would have no problem murdering someone in order to get wealthy," Julie suggested.

"He does have an arrogance about him, and he definitely thinks he is smarter than the rest of us," Myrtle agreed.

"He's also the right age to be a grandson of a bad seed. He could have gone into the dressing room to steal the scarf, and then accidentally kill Jan while fighting him for the scarf," I mused.

"I did hear Cindy tell Theresa on several occasions that she doesn't like him," Rhonda added.

Myrtle nodded for me to type the director's name into my phone. "That's good. Anton is a keeper. Who else should be on our list?"

"The police did interview Rene Vlught because he's the grandson of one of the bad seeds. What if there were others in the audience that the police didn't notice?" I suggested.

"Jan's grandfather named three men, and if they all had kids who had kids, we could be talking about a whole lot of suspects. We know that Rene's granddad told him about the puzzle box containing a code, so we have to assume that at least some of the other relatives knew about it, too," Rhonda said.

Myrtle groaned. "If that's the case, then we could have a hundred suspects to sift through, not a handful."

I paused a moment, thinking through our options and realizing she was right. "Why don't we stick with the crew for now, and let the police sort out the audience. Even if Cindy gave us a copy of the audience members' names and contact information, it would take us days to reach out to everyone."

"And the chance that the killer would tell us the truth about their movements is pretty slim, anyway."

"You're right, Myrtle. Besides, this does seem like it was an opportunity murder, as in the killer saw their chance and took it." I noted that Julie was nodding along with me.

Rhonda threw up her hands. "For all we know, that gallery owner really did kill Jan. Just because the police released him doesn't mean he's innocent—only that they don't have enough evidence to hold him any longer."

"Okay, ladies, we're getting way off track. All I have so far is Theresa, Anton, Rene, or possibly another unnamed relative of the bad seeds. Anyone else?" I searched my fellow passengers' faces, but they all remained blank.

I cast my mind back to the taping and all who were present. There was one name we had not yet discussed. "What about the cameraman—Joris? He's a self-proclaimed WWII buff with an extensive knowledge of the resistance groups active in the Netherlands. Maybe he knows more than he's letting on."

Rhonda looked over at me, her eyebrows knitted together. "You mean the man who helped us translate the letters? But he seems so nice."

"That's the one. It's odd that he knew quite a bit about the resistance groups and their more daring actions, but not about the groups' use of coded messages."

"Maybe he simply didn't think to mention it. None of us knew that the scarf was encoded, until after it was stolen. Besides, he didn't have to help us out, but offered to do so."

I tapped my chin. "Maybe he offered to translate the letters because he is also looking for clues to the treasure's location."

"Why are we even discussing this? It couldn't have been Joris because he would have been manning his camera during the taping," Rhonda said.

"He was, but something went wrong with his camera's feed at the end of the show. I saw him and Anton messing with the cables," I reasoned.

I thought back to that fateful moment, a few minutes before the lights shorted out. He and the director were fiddling with the wires attached to Joris's camera. Because they couldn't fix whatever was wrong, he'd followed Anton back to the monitor bay. Or at least, he had followed the director behind the curtain shielding the audience from backstage. Whether he had actually followed the director to the monitor bay was unclear.

"But they couldn't fix it, and I saw him leave his station and go backstage before the lights went out."

Myrtle rolled her eyes. "I think you're overanalyzing things, but put Joris on the list, if you want. But now that you mention it, Joris did translate the letters for us while we were inside the church. Who else could have heard us talking about the contents of the letters?"

"Gosh, most of the crew, I suspect. The audience was kept separate, but that doesn't mean that they couldn't have heard something. The acoustics in old churches are rather funky," Rhonda said.

Mention of the photos of Jan's letters reminded me of another set of images we'd used to follow the trail Jan's grandfather had laid. "Rhonda, when you took those photos of the scarf, the night before the show, was anyone else around?"

Rhonda snorted. "Yeah, lots of people. The crew was setting up the stage, and Cindy and Anton were fighting about the lighting. It wasn't a secret that I was trying to open the box. I don't know who exactly saw me, but any member of the crew could have seen me take pictures of it."

Myrtle hit the steering wheel with the palm of her hand. "Darn it, that means we're back to square one. We don't know who did it, or if they're already recovered whatever Jan's granddad hid away."

"Assuming he did hide something away," Julie reminded us.

"Someone killed Jan, so I'm guessing there is a treasure to be found," I countered.

"Wait a second, Carmen. Even if someone has already decoded the scarf, we have the key, not Jan's killer!" Rhonda clapped her hands together in delight.

I pulled the key out of my pocket. "Which means they probably can't access the artwork, or whatever Jan's granddad hid away."

Julie and I locked eyes, smiling as we did. "Which means we may have an advantage over our scarf thief."

I shouldn't have been so smug, I know, but it did feel good to have a leg up on our competition. Now that we knew what the scarf really was and what it may lead to, I couldn't help but feel the thrill of adventure rising up inside of me.

Apparently my bestie's head was filled with the same thoughts. "Now we really do have to follow the trail and solve the mystery! What do you think we're going to find at the end of the trail?"

"If the rumors are true, then I suspect artwork, and lots of it. The letter mentioned that he'd stolen a shipment," Myrtle said.

"What kind of art do you think we'll find? Wouldn't it be incredible if there's a Vermeer or Rembrandt inside?" Rhonda said dreamily.

I couldn't help but smile at the thought. "That would be pretty amazing. But they might not be by famous artists at all," I added, unintentionally bursting Rhonda's bubble.

"Whatever it is, it was valuable to someone, if they went to all that trouble to hide it away from the Nazis," Myrtle said.

"Would you look at that windmill?" Rhonda suddenly exclaimed, as she pointed to a colorful one racing past our window. Myrtle seemed to be channeling Dutch Formula One champion Max Verstappen today, and we were getting a rapid view of the Netherlands.

The speedy scenery distracted us all from the suspect list, which was fine considering there was no one else to add to it. Our named suspect list wasn't long, but those on it did have a valid reason to want to get their hands on Jan's puzzle box. Or, rather, whatever lay at the end of the trail—if such a trail even existed. After our conversation tapered off and Julie and Rhonda began chatting about places they wanted to visit together, I leaned my head against the window, wondering where this chase would lead us.

22

Old Wounds

Shortly after our conversation about the suspects died out, Rhonda and Julie's conversation grew quiet, and soon both were softly snoring. I should have figured the rocking motion of the van would put the pair to sleep.

I'd been hoping to talk to Myrtle about Mac's phone since she arrived, but there had been something in the way every chance I got. It didn't help that I didn't want Rhonda or my partner to know that I was actively tracking my husband's killer. But now that I could hear Julie and Rhonda sleeping, I figured it was a good moment to ask.

"Say, Myrtle, how are you doing with cracking Mac's phone?" I asked in a voice soft enough not to disturb the others.

Without making eye contact, Myrtle replied evenly, "My team deciphered it a week ago. I have it with me and am authorized to give it back to you during this trip."

I shot forward to look her in the eye. "Wait a second. You've had it with you this whole time and haven't said a word about it? You know I've been riding Reggie to crack it open."

"Yes, I do. But we needed you to keep your head in the recovery game until your last assignment was finished."

I eyed her massive purse. "Do you have it on your person?"

"Yes." Without another word, Myrtle plunged one hand into her bag and dug around until she found it.

I stared at Mac's phone. "Unbelievable." My irritation level was sky-high, but I knew from experience that sarcastic remarks only made Myrtle clam up.

"Yes, well, I didn't really get the chance to pull you aside and talk to you about this earlier, did I? Things have been action-packed since you returned to Amsterdam."

I grabbed the phone and took in Mac's screen saver, a picture of a tiny bulldog puppy with his tongue lolling out of his mouth. I hadn't pegged Mac for a dog lover. Now that I had it in my hands, I wondered what I would discover about Antonio Corozza, Esmerelda Bianci, and my father.

"Have you had a chance to read through the contents of Mac's phone?"

Myrtle sighed deeply. "Yes, and we only found a few references to Antonio Corozza, but no direct way of contacting him. I'm afraid the guy you lifted it off of was not as highly placed as he made himself out to be."

I could feel my blood pressure rising. "Are you certain? Have you really gone through all of his messages and files, or are you trying to blow me off?"

Myrtle paused for a moment, as if to ensure that I really heard her words. "Carmen, there's nothing linking Antonio to Mac on it. Nothing at all. He was taking orders from a midlevel gangster named Marcello, who is associated with Corozza's organization, but is by no means highly placed. I'm afraid Mac was bluffing, if he said he was in direct contact with Antonio."

"No, that can't be." I held my fists against my temple, not wanting to accept Myrtle's words.

"My team has gone through everything with a fine-tooth comb. I put my best men on it because Reggie wants to find Carlos's killer as much as you do. Not only is Antonio a dangerous criminal sought by pretty much every law enforcement agency in Europe and the United States, Carlos was killed while on assignment for the Rosewood Agency. Trust me, Reggie wants to see Antonio brought to justice for all the wrong he has done. But he doesn't want to lose you in the process—neither one of us does. That's why we want to continue focusing on hurting his network, and thereby him, without any more of our agents coming into his crosshairs."

I threw my head back, wanting to howl in frustration. This was not what I had expected to find out. Yet when I thought back on Mac's threats, I realized that he had not said that he had direct contact with Antonio, only implied it. "I really thought his phone would get us closer to Antonio."

"I'm sorry, kid, but it doesn't look like it. But let's be honest, even if you knew where he was, the chance of you getting close enough to actually harm him physically is pretty much zero. And if you did manage to stab or shoot him, his bodyguards would shoot you dead before you could get away."

Myrtle grabbed my arm and squeezed. "I know you want him to tell you why he killed Carlos, even though you know the answer. Carlos's cover must have been blown, and he was murdered as a result."

I took in her words, wondering whether she was on to something. The painful blinding truth was that Myrtle was right. There was no chance of me getting close enough to Antonio to kill him, and the chance of surviving was pretty much zero. Was risking my life worth knowing why Carlos had to die?

In the days right after Carlos's death, the answer would have been a resounding yes. But time did heal all wounds—even the festering ones—and four years later, my obsession with knowing the truth about Carlos's last few minutes on this earth was beginning to fade.

I didn't need to confront the mob boss to know what happened to my husband. I could easily imagine what had occurred when Antonio had found Carlos on his yacht, searching for two stolen statues. If Antonio hadn't shot him, one of his henchmen had. I suppose I clung to the belief that hearing Antonio say those words aloud would provide me with some sort of closure. Without a body to bury, it was still difficult to accept that Carlos was well and truly gone.

Myrtle kept her eyes on the road. I had a sneaking suspicion it wasn't because she was being a careful driver, but that she was avoiding eye contact. Yet I had more questions I needed her to answer.

"Do you recognize the name Dottoressa Esmerelda Bianci? She may have popped up in Mac's phone conversations."

Although Bianci seemed like a sweet little old lady who was scared of Antonio, it would not be the first time a granny tried to lay a trap for me.

And I was still not entirely certain that the Antonio I was searching for was even the same one she mentioned.

Myrtle thought a moment. "Nope, sorry."

"And what about Carmino Corozza?" My voice was a whisper. I knew Myrtle did not know that he was my father, but it still felt strange asking about him.

She shook her head. "That name doesn't ring any bells, either. Is it Antonio's son? His daughters are mentioned a few times, but no one named Carmino, as far as I can recall."

"This is highly disappointing," I said, as neutrally as possible, despite the overwhelming sense of despair her words caused to well up within me. I had pinned my hopes on it containing more intel. After weeks of anticipation, hearing that the phone contained nothing useful was a crushing blow.

"Look, I know you're not pleased, but I see no reason to lie to you about it, either. You have the phone and can scour it yourself now, if you don't believe me. But Carmen, there is something else you need to know first. Interpol is also attempting to infiltrate Antonio's network, because of another case. Dave's boss at Interpol contacted Reggie to ask if Rosewood had any useful intel we were willing to share. Reggie had me send over every file we had, including a copy of the contents of Mac's phone. Which means we can let them find and capture Antonio for us. It keeps you safe and still accomplishes our end goal of seeing Antonio pay for his crimes."

My mind was reeling with possibilities. I had to get myself placed onto that team. "Is Dave the team leader?"

"I don't know for certain. We didn't discuss the details. But I do know Interpol is coordinating with several law enforcement agencies for this one."

I wondered whether that was the case Dave was about to start working on. Maybe I would give him a ring, after all. "Whatever Interpol is planning, I want in on it."

"Whoa, that's not our call to make. It sounds like a big operation with lots of chefs in the kitchen, if you know what I mean."

My determined expression caused Myrtle's tone to lose its certainty. "Reggie can try. After helping Dave wrap up the Silver Fox case, you do have an in."

"Let's leverage that."

"Okay, but can you let it go for now, at least until we've sorted out this current situation? I need your head in this game, too."

"Trust me, I'm happy to. I want to see where this leads as much as you do. I just hope we can figure out what the encoded message means before Jan's murderer does."

"I bet we're way ahead of the killer. Joris is a self-proclaimed WWII buff, and even he didn't think of the scarf containing Morse code," Myrtle added.

"You make a good point," I answered automatically, yet her statement got me thinking. "Why didn't Joris tell us about the resistance groups using encoded messages? He should have known about that. Did he forgot to mention it, or did he truly not know? Or did he intentionally not mention it because he was the one who stole the scarf?"

Myrtle chuckled. "Man, you go dark quick. Joris sure seems like a sincere and helpful guy. But experience has taught me that anyone can be a killer, if the right circumstances present themselves."

"Or the wrong ones," I murmured.

Myrtle nodded to the rearview mirror. "I hate to change the subject, but we've had someone on our tail since we left Amsterdam. I thought we shook him at the gas station, but he's back."

I scanned the side and rearview mirrors, looking for anything suspicious. "What? Where?"

"It's the red Mazda with a dent in the hood. Three cars back on our left."

"Shoot, I can't see who's driving."

"Me, either. I tried to get closer to them earlier, but could only get a glimpse of the driver in my mirror. They slowed down when I did and changed lanes so I couldn't get right up next to them. I only saw one person in the vehicle. Based on their posture, I would bet it's a man. But they are wearing a wide-brimmed hat and sunglasses, so it's hard to be certain. Maybe it's nothing, but let's keep our guard up, shall we?"

"Agreed. I wonder if it's a friend of one of the bad seeds."

"It could very well be, especially if their profiteering grandparents had told them about the missing art."

I sighed and glanced out the window again as a windmill raced by. "I hope the police were able to find another lead to Jan's killer."

"I'm certain the police are still processing all of those interviews and any evidence found at the crime scene. With a little luck, they'll find a fingerprint or other piece of evidence pointing to his murderer. And if not, we might just figure out why he was killed. That may help the police solve their case."

Myrtle nodded in agreement as she glanced in the rearview mirror again. "Say, we're about ten minutes away from Hazelbroek. I'm going to try to shake our tail one more time before we arrive. Could you wake up our sleeping beauties?"

23

Tracking Down A Lead

When Myrtle turned onto the main road heading into town, I couldn't help but sigh. Whatever I had been expecting, this wasn't it. We rode slowly past rows of small, identical homes and through a smattering of shops and cafes, all built in concrete and brick. Only a handful of lone souls shuffled along the sidewalks.

"Quite the bustling town here, isn't it?" The sarcasm that dripped from Myrtle's voice made it clear that she agreed with my silent assessment of the place.

We were soon at the center of the village. A few main roads radiated out from a circular-shaped square, from which locals could easily access a rather spartan church, a town hall built from concrete slabs, and a large grocery store. I had expected the cute Dutch architecture typical of most of the towns I had been in, not these modern, soulless boxes. "I bet most of the town was destroyed during the war. That would explain the predominantly post-war architecture."

"I hope that doesn't make it harder for us to find the location the scarf was referring to. What if the Westerstraete home was destroyed during the war, too?" Myrtle moaned.

"Don't give up hope just yet. I bet someone in this town knows the Westerstraete family. We just have to figure out where they live now. Maybe we should try asking around at the grocery store," Rhonda replied.

"That's a great idea. However, we may have more luck at City Hall. It's right over there. Their archivist should be able to search their records for us," I said.

My traveling companions looked to where I was pointing. "It does look like they are open. Why don't we ask?" Myrtle suggested, as if it was her own idea.

I chuckled to myself as Rhonda, Julie and I followed Myrtle towards the entrance to City Hall. The receptionist led us over to their archivist, a nice elderly volunteer who seemed to be absently flipping through a magazine when we approached.

When Myrtle asked about the Westerstraete family and specifically any relatives that may still be alive, she startled slightly, but searched the city's database, nonetheless.

Several seconds later, we hit our first roadblock.

"I'm sorry, but we have no families with that name in our records, and they date back two hundred years."

"Great. So we're at a dead end after all," Julie said, disappointment ringing though her voice. "Sorry, Mom."

As we turned to walk away, the archivist cleared her throat quite loudly, making us all turn back.

"Are you certain Westerstraete is a family name?" she asked.

I leaned onto the counter. "To be honest, we are not. Why do you ask?"

"There's an old house with that name on the outskirts of town. The last owners left it to the city decades ago, and it's been a cultural center and public park ever since. Did you know two Jewish families were hidden away in the attic, during the Second World War? The caretaker has a memory like an elephant. I don't know what or who you're looking for exactly, but if it's got anything to do with that house, he may be able to help."

"That's really kind of you, thanks. Could you show me where it is?" I opened my phone's map before handing it to the archivist. She typed the address in, adding, "The arts center is usually open in the morning for workshops, and you can park your car for free around the back."

We bade her goodbye and piled back into the van, all agreeing that this was a promising lead. But our enthusiasm was immediately curbed when we reached the estate. The name Westerstraete was indeed woven into the imposing gate. But as we drove down a long driveway flanked by a large grassy park and into the parking lot, I noted that the house appeared to be locked up tight.

Once Myrtle had parked, I sprung out and rushed over to the doors. They were indeed locked, and when I cupped my hands over the glass panes, I could see that the lights were out. The rest joined me eventually, albeit at a slower pace.

"It's closed. We'll have to try to track down the caretaker. Maybe the receptionist at City Hall knows how to contact them."

I started to turn back to the van, when Rhonda said, "Since we're here, why don't we take a minute to stretch our legs? It looks so pretty here, with all of those statues and little ponds."

"Great idea, Mom. After that long drive, I would like that, too," Julie added.

"Okay, that sounds good, actually." My legs were a bit cramped, as well.

Myrtle and I followed mother and daughter, now walking hand in hand, towards the park's main path. On one side of the house was a pleasant grass-filled park with lots of water features, tiny bridges, and many statues. There were practically no visitors, and the grounds were so extensive, it felt as if we had the place to ourselves. When I stood still, I could hear the birds singing and even nearby squirrels foraging for nuts.

Julie stopped in front of a statue of a young boy holding a ball in one hand. A cocker spaniel danced at his feet. I stood next to her, impressed by how well the artist had captured both the dog's joy and boy's expressive grin in metal.

In contrast to a typical French or English garden, the statues were not of Greek or Roman gods, but a collection of children and dogs. At first I thought it was simply the artist's specialty, until I noted that memorial plaques were attached to most of the pedestals, with the names of the children and animals portrayed.

"Wow, the family that lived here must have been loaded to have commissioned all of these statues!" Julie exclaimed.

"They certainly are adorable," her mother added.

"It's too bad they aren't gods," Myrtle grumbled. "That would have explained the Atlas reference."

Her words sparked an idea in my brain. "Wait a second—maybe we aren't looking for a god, but the name of a child or animal. Let's spread out and check all of the memorial plaques for anything named Atlas."

"Great thinking!" Myrtle called out before jogging towards the statues farthest from us.

A few minutes later, Rhonda cried out, "Over here!" She stood before a statue of a young girl and her dog. The hound had a collar on, and from it hung a small globe. "In loving memory of Atlas" was inscribed onto the memorial plaque. I dug my heel into the ground, glad I was wearing thick-soled wedges. A wide patch of earth moved with my foot.

"The ground is so sandy, we might be able to dig into it. Everyone look around; maybe we can find a stick or something strong enough to dig with."

Rhonda gasped. "But what if someone sees us?"

"There aren't that many people around, and I don't see any security cameras pointed out to the garden, only the house. We've come this far, so we should see this through. Wait a second—there might be something in the van we can use. I'll go check."

Sure enough, there was a small foldup shovel tucked into an extensive emergency kit that would satisfy any survivalist.

The others formed a loose circle around me as I furiously flicked tiny shovels full of sandy dirt away, digging into the ground under the dog's collar.

When I reached fifteen fists deep, more or less, I hit metal.

"Bingo!" I grinned over at my companions.

"Oh, that sounds promising! Be careful, Carmen. We don't want to accidentally break anything," Rhonda cried out.

"But don't move too slowly, otherwise someone might see what we're doing," Myrtle chastised.

I looked around but only saw a few crows watching us, probably hoping I'd turn up a few worms for an easy meal, while digging.

Still, I leaned down and brushed my hand over the surface. A smooth piece of metal was my reward. I kept pushing the sandy dirt away until I could see what appeared to be the lid of a small metal box. It only took a few more scoops to free it because the ground was surprisingly loose and easy to dig through. Which was a good thing. The art center was closed, but that didn't mean other visitors couldn't be wandering around the grounds or that the caretaker wouldn't show up.

Once it was completely exposed, I leaned down and pulled it out, admiring our find. It was about the size of a cigar box and made of metal. I noted that the lid didn't seem to be locked in any way. Just as I dropped my shovel, with the intention of opening the lid, Myrtle nudged me. "Grab your shovel and let's get that back to the van. Now scoot!"

24

Shaking Their Tail

While we walked back to the van, I couldn't help but think of how easy it had been to dig up the box.

"Don't you think it was odd that the soil was so loose? If it had been buried there since the war, I would have expected it to be rock hard."

"What are you grousing about? That grass bed looked pretty new. For all we know, they recently scraped off the topsoil and replaced it with sod. If that was the case, we're lucky they didn't go fifteen fists deep, otherwise the groundskeeper would have found this box."

"This whole thing feels too easy. Don't you think it's strange that we located this box so quickly? The scarf was pretty simple to decipher once we figured out that it was Morse code," I pushed. Maybe Myrtle was right, but I couldn't help but feel that it was all too simple. Maybe it was because we had missed an important clue, or perhaps because I was used to having to work harder to solve a mystery.

As we walked back towards our vehicle, the rain clouds that had been threatening since we'd arrived slowly began to drizzle. I looked up to the skies, glad I'd dug up the box before the rain had kicked in.

"If it was too difficult of a code, it might never have been found," Rhonda countered. "You know, like that treasure that's been supposedly been buried on Oak Island for the past two-hundred-something years? Jan's granddad did leave the box behind for his son, presumably so he could find whatever is at the end of this trail."

"I suppose…" I couldn't quite shake the feeling that it wasn't just the code's simplicity that was important, yet I could not tell the others why. And they were simply pleased that we had found the next clue so quickly.

"You're seeing things, Carmen; be happy that we were smart enough to puzzle the code out so quickly. Right, ladies?" Myrtle high-fived Julie and Rhonda.

When she turned back around, Myrtle gulped audibly. "Uh, oh. Carmen, we may have a problem."

She slowed to a halt, causing the rest of us to do the same, then nodded to a red Mazda with a dented hood parked across from our van. I studied the hood and license plate. "That's the car that's been tailing us since Amsterdam, isn't it?"

"I believe it is."

I squinted to try to see through the front window, but whoever was behind the wheel was squished down into the driver's seat to the point that I could only see the top of a black hoodie. The drizzle didn't help with visibility. Luckily for us, I could see that their head was turned towards our van and not the parking lot.

I handed Rhonda the box and shovel. "Myrtle, could you give Julie the keys? Why don't you and your mom slowly walk over to the van and get in. Myrtle and I are going to see who's driving."

"Sure thing. Come on, Mom." Julie grabbed her mother's hand, and the pair did as I'd asked.

Myrtle nodded her approval as she slid up next to me. "Good thinking, Carmen. I'll take the passenger's side and let you approach the driver's door. Ready?" While mother and daughter sauntered towards the van and hopefully distracted the driver, Myrtle and I hunched down and weaved back around the pickup truck parked next to the Mazda, before splitting up. Myrtle crouched around the trunk while I slunk over to the driver's door. I peeked inside through the rear window. There was a person behind the wheel, but the hoodie made it impossible to tell whether it was a man or a woman, let alone identify them.

I counted to three and pulled on the driver's door handle, hoping it was unlocked. Sure enough, it was, and when the driver turned to face me, my jaw dropped open in shock.

"Anton Berhard! Why are you following us?"

The director of *Antiques Time* held his hands up, as if I was holding a gun to his head. When Myrtle sprung up and glared at him through the window, he shrieked.

"I'm sorry if I frightened you. It was not my intention. I just wanted to see what you'd find."

I rocked back on my heels, using the doorframe to steady me. "What do you mean?"

Anton blew out his cheeks yet remained silent.

I glared at him as best as I could. "Don't play coy with me. All I have to do is make one phone call and the cops will be after you for Jan's murder."

Anton's eyes shot open. "I didn't kill him! It's nothing like that. I saw Rhonda take pictures of the scarf after she'd figured out how to open it at the studio. Later, I overheard you and Joris talking about Jan's letters and how his granddad had hidden something away. After I saw you take that puzzle box out of the dressing room, I figured you were after the art Rene Vlught mentioned. So I followed you down here to see where you'd go."

"You mean to steal whatever we find, right?"

"No! I want to film the story, not commit a crime. I am a documentary maker, after all."

His irritation was so extreme, I found myself inclined to believe him. "What exactly do you want to film?"

"I'm between projects and thought Jan's grandfather being in the resistance and the rumors about his missing puzzle box might make a fascinating film. These kinds of espionage stories are still quite popular in the Netherlands, and I'm certain the local public would want to see it. 'Encoded scarf leads to missing treasure trove' would make a great tagline for the commercials."

"How did you know about the scarf being encoded? Jan didn't mention it on the show." I had trouble keeping the surprise out of my voice.

"The use of codes during WWII is fairly well known, especially among history buffs. Anyone interested in WWII would think to check the scarf for an encoded message, especially if it had been hidden away like that. I figured that was why someone killed Jan, to get ahold of the scarf."

Anton studied my face, smiling in delight. "I was right—it is in Morse code, isn't it?"

"I knew it," I hissed to Myrtle. "Joris was holding back on us. But why?"

Anton mistook my tone as disappointment with his answer. He slammed his hands onto the steering wheel. "I'm telling you the truth—I only wanted to make a documentary about the puzzle box."

I studied him critically, but the arrogant jut of his chin didn't sit well with me. "I still don't believe you. Who's to say you didn't kill Jan for the scarf?"

"If I had, why would I be following you?"

"To get ahold of the key that was still hidden in the puzzle box." It was a risky move, telling him about the key, but I had to see his reaction.

"Are you serious? Wow, this story is getting better by the minute. I had no idea that there was a key inside of the box. I swear. How did you figure that out?" The way his jaw dropped open, I'd have to say he was telling the truth.

I glared at him, unwilling to trust him quite yet. "Step out of the car."

When he did as I asked, I herded him towards the back of his Mazda where Myrtle was waiting, then held out my hand. "Give me your keys."

"Why?"

"Because I'm going to call the cops and don't want you driving off before they get here."

When he grimaced, I cocked my head at him. "If you are telling the truth, then you have no reason to run. Myrtle, keep an eye on him, will you?"

"You bet." She folded her arms over her torso, a steely glint in her eye. Glad to have one problem resolved, I pulled out my phone to deal with another. As I dialed the number of the investigator leading Jan's murder investigation, I couldn't help but wonder whether he would take me seriously this time, or blow me off as a nosy busybody again.

While waiting for the call to connect, I paced towards the hood of the Mazda, trying to release some of my nervous energy. A scuffling noise behind me made me turn back in time to see Anton shooting past Myrtle.

She raced after him, clocking a pretty good speed, but still not fast enough to catch up with the Dutchman. I hung up and followed after them, but was too far behind to have real chance at grabbing Anton. He shot across the street, almost getting hit by a car, before disappearing into a residential neighborhood.

"Is it worth racing after him?" Myrtle panted.

I studied the street, realizing that there were many opportunities for him to jump a garden fence or hide under any of the cars parked along the street. "No, we have his keys, and he doesn't know where we are headed next. Which means he won't be able to follow us. That's all that matters right now. But I should call this in anyway, just so the lead investigator knows to check Anton out."

"Let's open the box first. It may be worth sharing the contents with the police, as well," Myrtle urged.

I looked to the phone in my hand, considering my options. Truth be told, I couldn't wait to see what was inside, either. And as long as Anton couldn't follow us, there was no rush to track him down. "You're right. Let's get back to the van."

25

Message Inscribed In Stone

Once Myrtle caught her breath, we joined Julie and Rhonda in the back of the van, the metal box placed between them. After we slid the door closed, Rhonda ran her hand along the lip-shaped handle. "It's not even padlocked, though there's a ring where one is clearly meant to go."

I looked over her shoulder to examine the lid. "After all the trouble Jan's granddad went through to hide the thing, I expected it to be more secure." I touched the key in my pocket. If it wasn't meant to open this box, what was it meant for?

Rhonda held out the box to her daughter. "Julie, honey, why don't you do the honors."

"Thanks, Mom." She set it on her lap and tugged twice before the lid opened. "Oh, my. This is pretty biblical."

She turned the box so we could all see the contents. Inside was a stone table with an inscription etched into its surface. Julie tried to read the words aloud, but it was in Dutch.

"Let me take a look." I leaned over and transcribed the message into my phone, before reading the English version aloud. "One kilometer from Velsen Windmill to the Green Cathedral. Under the branches of the intertwining trees."

The van fell silent for a moment while we all processed the cryptic message.

"Are you sure you translated that right?" Myrtle finally asked.

"I think so. I'll run it again." A second later, the refreshed version appeared. "Same thing. Well, I guess our next move is to see if we can find a windmill named Velsen, preferably one in the vicinity."

Second later Julie held her phone up in triumph. "Got it! This must be the one—it's only a few miles away from here. According to this satellite image, the Velsen Windmill is located across from the town square of Vredesdijk, at the entrance of a large park that appears to be heavily forested."

I strained to get a better look at the tiny map. "Where is it exactly?"

"It looks to be a ten-minute drive." She looked up at us with a gleam in her eye. "I say we check this out."

Before I could agree, Rhonda spoke up. "It sounds like quite a few people saw Carmen sneak off with the puzzle box. If Anton has been following us this whole time, someone else may also be. Someone killed Jan to find whatever his granddad hid away, and I don't want any of us to be next. I would never be able to forgive myself if anything horrible happened to you." Rhonda grabbed her daughter's hand as her eyes welled up.

"Mom's right. If Anton and Theresa saw Carmen take the box, anyone could have. And it sounds like several crew members saw Mom photograph the scarf, as well," Julie said.

"Only those working in the studio that night," Rhonda rushed to add.

"Hold on a second. Anton was driving the car I saw following us, and I didn't see anyone else on our tail. It should be safe to continue," Myrtle reasoned, but her tone was a touch less enthusiastic.

However, that key was burning a hole in my pocket. I was itching to see what it opened, and what lay inside. "But whoever took the scarf must not have been able to decode the message, otherwise the box under Atlas's globe wouldn't have been there, right?" I said, though once the words were out, I questioned my own reasoning. Was that true? Not necessarily.

Before I could speak up, Myrtle groused, "What does it matter? We do have the key, after all."

Rhonda crinkled up her nose. "That's exactly what I mean. Whoever took the scarf is still missing the key, and no one knows how far that person is willing to go to get ahold of it. I think we should tell the investigating officer about this lead, just in case someone is still following us. Think of it as backup. If he refuses to do anything about it, we still can. But at least he'll know where we're at and what we're up to."

I blew out my cheeks. The Amsterdam police seemed to see me more as a nuisance than as a helper, and I wondered how the lead detective would react to my latest news. Yet I knew if I didn't call him, Rhonda would most likely refuse to leave the van again and forbid Julie from helping us, as well.

I pulled out my phone. "Okay, you win. I'll call the detective."

26

Upsetting The Detective

I dialed as requested, then waited quite a while to be connected to the lead detective. Part of me wondered whether he was hoping I would hang up first. As soon as he picked up, I launched into a detailed explanation of how we had followed the scarf's trail to Hazelbroek, as well as our suspicions about the director—figuring he would want to know everything. Yet my desire to do the right thing was tempered quite quickly, once the inspector got a word in.

"My team is still sorting through all of the witness statements and we are not yet ready to entertain your theories about any missing artwork. We are spread thin as it is. I've told you before, the murder is our priority. For all I know, you killed Jan for the scarf. You do seem obsessed with finding the artwork," he barked.

"Why would I call you, if that was true?" I countered, knowing he really didn't suspect me of murder, otherwise I would be in the station being interviewed right now. But he was clearly harried. I could only imagine how much overtime he was going to have to work, in order to solve this case.

"I don't know, to see how far we are with the investigation. Or to waste our time, so that it takes us longer to pin this crime on you."

I had to stifle a snort. "Can't you call someone local and ask them to check the location in the park for the missing art?"

"All you have is a set of clues leading you from a windmill to a church. You don't even know where exactly to look, or whether there is something to be found. Tell you what, if you do find something out there, call the local police department yourself," he said gruffly. "I don't even know where you are."

"Neither do we," I admitted.

"Then why are you wasting my time?" He hung up before I could answer.

Granted, he did sound agitated. But that was not a valid excuse to discount me as a nosy busybody or our information as nonsense.

I laid my phone down in my lap and turned to the others. "Well, ladies, it looks like we're on our own. The inspector is not interested—at least, not unless we actually find a missing masterpiece. We can call the local cops, but I doubt they will take action, either," I concluded, after relaying all that the inspector had said.

"So what are we going to do?"

Julie turned to Rhonda and took her mother's hands in hers. "I know you're concerned about our safety, but it sounds like if we don't search for this location, no one else will. We've come this far—I would like to know if Jan's granddad did hide something away. Especially if it helps the police bring his killer to justice. Even if they don't believe the two are related, it sure seems like he was murdered for whatever is buried under that Green Cathedral."

"I'm with Julie. We should keep following the trail and see if we can find the art. If we do, we can call the local police," Myrtle said.

"I agree. What do you think, Rhonda? Do you want to join us or wait in the van?" I looked to Rhonda, wondering which way she was going to go.

My bestie only pursed her lips. "I don't really have a choice, do I? I'll only worry myself to death if I stay behind. I'm in."

"Then it's settled. Let me get us the directions. Myrtle, do you want to drive or should I?"

My company contact swiped the keys out of Julie's hand. "I've got this."

27

In Search Of A Windmill

When Myrtle pulled into the parking lot, I took a moment to study our surroundings. The park's entrance was on one side of the town square and seemed to designate the edge of town. It shared a parking lot with a church and an ice cream parlor, both currently closed. Unfortunately, the church was neither green nor a cathedral, but rather a Presbyterian house of worship. On the other side of the church began a row of quaint brick buildings, with shops on the ground floor and apartments on the two floors above. Most appeared to be closed, save for a few cafes whose lights shone bright, farther down the road.

The lot was half full when we pulled in, but before we could park, the storm that had been threatening us all afternoon broke loose in a torrent, drenching everyone in the rain's path. We parked as close as we could to the trailhead, a short stretch of concrete that led to the park's entrance.

The sudden burst of rain had dog walkers and Lycra-wearing joggers rushing back up the trail to their vehicles *en masse*. Despite the weather, the windmill was easy to spot, its wooden blades rising high above the surrounding tree line.

I peered out of the van's window and up at the dark gray skies. We hadn't been expecting a torrential storm, so none of us had brought rain gear. "Hmm, that may take a while. I don't see any blue out there."

"Should we wait for the skies to clear?" Rhonda asked.

"We've come too far to wait around any longer. There's a map of the park over on that information board. Maybe the Green Cathedral's location is listed on it, too. I'm going to take a look," Myrtle declared before she threw the van's door open and sprung out of the driver's seat, her jean jacket over her head.

We all watched her sprint over to an information board and study the map on it.

"Myrtle's right, there's no point in waiting. Let's go, Mom."

"But my hair!"

"Come on, Rhonda, we can use our vests as umbrellas."

I grabbed my jacket and opened the door, letting a flood of rain inside, then jumped out. My cotton vest was no match for the downpour and did little to protect my head or hair. A narrow roof over the map did not offer shelter for the four of us, but did make it easier to read. Only once I'd had a chance to study the map did I realize the scale of it all. It wasn't a few short trails meandering around an artificial lake, but a fairly large and heavily forested area. It would take us hours to walk all of the trails. Hopefully, we wouldn't have to.

The information board showed the map of the park, and also explained its history in Dutch, German, French, and English. During WWII, several ammunition bunkers and defense forts had been built in this area, but most had been left standing to rot where they were. Some of the underground bunkers' entrances were hard to see thanks to the shrubbery, which was why visitors were advised to stay on the marked trails, or risk accidentally falling into an old bunker.

"There are bunkers here; that's a great sign. Joris did say that the Klavers hid their artwork underground," I said, taking in the information, feeling like we were on the right path.

Myrtle tapped the trailhead on the map. "There are three main paths leading through the park that all form a loop. But I don't see any mention of a Green Cathedral or any intertwining trees on here. Even if the church was in ruins, you would think it would be noted on the map."

"Shoot, I bet these paths are post-war. A lot must have changed since 1945,"

Rhonda groused.

I studied the map as well. Myrtle was right in that the trails all looped back around to the entrance, but they went off in three directions—left, right, and straight behind the windmill. Without knowing where that cathedral was, we could easily walk around aimlessly for hours and still not find it.

"What now? Should we split up?" Julie asked.

"We would cover ground faster that way," Myrtle agreed.

"I don't like that idea one bit. If we're going to look for this bunker, we are sticking together," Rhonda demanded.

I spied a dog walker coming up the trail towards the car park. "Or we can ask a local."

Before the others could react, I bolted over to the young woman speed walking towards her car, her jacket over her head and a terrier in tow.

I cupped my hands over my eyes so I could see her face. "I'm so sorry to bother you, but we're looking for a pair of intertwining trees close to the Green Cathedral. Do you know if either one is in this park?" I didn't even bother asking whether she could speak English. Except for the oldest generation, everyone in this country spoke my native language fluently.

She looked at me curiously for a moment. "Yes, I do. But why are you asking?"

When I showed her the Dutch version of the message, typed into my phone, her face lit up in a grin. "Is this one of those treasure hunts the local tourist board has organized for expats—to get to know the area better? I read about it in the local news."

I smiled widely, not knowing what she meant, but playing along anyway. "Yes, as a matter of fact, it is. It's a great idea. I'm really enjoying learning more about Limburg."

She beamed, clearly pleased with my answer and enthusiasm. "You must be enjoying it, if you're out in this weather. I don't know about the intertwining trees, but I know where the Green Cathedral is. Follow the center path, starting behind the windmill. It curves around a bit, but you should reach the grove of trees in about fifteen minutes."

Her words caught me off-guard. "Wait a second, it's not a church, but a group of trees?"

She laughed. "Yes, it sounds like the tourist office is making certain you talk to locals while you're solving these puzzles. You would have to ask someone who lives here to know where the Green Cathedral is, so that was smart of them. It's an old cluster of trees whose canopies have grown so intertwined in a pitched roof pattern that it appears to be a church roof from a distance."

She briefly held her hands together in a steeple, before protecting her head again.

A wave of relief flowed over me. "That's wonderful information—thank you so much, we appreciate it."

When a clap of thunder sounded, we both jerked our heads up. "I'm heading home. Good luck with your hunt—and don't forget to study Dutch!" The woman waved as she jogged to her car, her dog in tow.

I returned to the others and relayed the woman's directions, before heading back to the van to grab the foldup shovel. We didn't know in which direction we should be looking, but if the artwork had been hidden away for so many decades, my bet was that it was underground. And if it had remained undiscovered all of this time, the entrance was probably hidden.

We started down the well-used path leading us through a thinly wooded area with lots of undergrowth. The first few hundred feet were paved, but soon the asphalt stopped, and the trail became gravel and dirt. The rainstorm had turned the trails to mud, garnering complaints from Rhonda about the state of her Prada heels.

The farther we traveled, the thicker the trees became, as did the shrubbery growing underneath. We passed a few hardcore joggers and a smattering of dog walkers, but I suspected the continuous rain had driven most away. On the one hand I was glad because that would give us more chances to find the art without being disturbed. On the other hand, if things went wrong, we were fairly isolated out here.

A few minutes in, we passed a dilapidated old WWII bunker on one side of the path. One half of the doorframe was all that remained of the entrance; the rest had fallen into the dark opening leading underground, blocking the ladder. I stopped to take in the exposed rusty bars sticking out of the crumbling asphalt, now being slowly broken down by tiny plants and moss.

"That's a good sign, don't you think?" I said as we walked past, our vests and jackets still over our heads.

"I suppose it is. I only hope that the bunker we are searching for is in better shape," Myrtle said.

I stared at the decrepit ruin. "Good point."

"How much farther do you think it is?" Rhonda asked.

I checked my watch. "We've been walking for eleven minutes, so you would think it would be right around the corner. I guess we should all start paying attention to the canopy growth."

Because of the thick undergrowth, trying to walk in a straight line from the windmill to the Green Cathedral was not really an option. Yet the way the path meandered back and forth was making it a challenge to track our distance. I had to hope that the local dog walker was right and that the cluster of trees would be obvious.

A sudden gust of wind brought another torrent of rain. Despite the intense showers, I couldn't shake the feeling that we were being watched. Yet whenever I scanned the surrounding trees, I couldn't see anyone. *It must be my nerves*, I figured, which was why I didn't say anything to the others. If I had, Rhonda would have certainly demanded that we abandon our search.

The farther we went, the fuller the trees appeared to be. We also caught sight of two more bunkers in ruins close to the trail. It felt like we were in the right place, but after twenty minutes, we still hadn't seen anything that resembled a cathedral. I was beginning to worry that we'd missed it, when all of a sudden we rounded another bend and I caught sight of it. Straight ahead was a grove of trees, their branches grown together so tightly, the ground underneath was practically dry. The tops of the canopies curved up on one side, reminding me of a church's bell tower. The foliage seemed to peak in the middle, like a steepled roof.

"There it is!" I screeched and ran for the clearing underneath the tightly woven canopy. In this rainstorm, it appeared to be the only dry spot left in the forest. Only a few drops had managed to get through the abundant foliage.

Once we were gathered under the canopy, we all looked up, taking in the grove of trees. "It's incredible. The branches are so thick, these trees must be quite old."

"This must be the Green Cathedral Jan's grandfather is referring to, don't you think?" I asked the others.

Myrtle slapped her hands together. "I concur. Let's see if we can find that pair of intertwining trees and solve this mystery."

"I hope this is where the art is. It might just hold another clue leading to a different location," Julie cautioned.

"The trees might be part of this Green Cathedral," I mused aloud, looked more closely at the trunks of the trees comprising the magnificent canopy. Alas, none were intertwined.

"It must be close by. Let's spread out and see if we can find it or them. I'll go left, Rhonda right, Myrtle straight ahead, and Julie can search behind us—is that good?"

"Sure thing!" Julie replied and set off in her assigned direction. "Good luck, everyone!"

The rest of us followed suit.

I grabbed the largest branch I could find and started trampling down the undergrowth. My wedges were definitely not made for mud or hiking, but I couldn't complain about the damage to my footwear, considering it was my harebrained idea to follow this trail.

I slowly walked forward, towards the next cluster of trees. To my disappointment, none seemed to be entwined. As I looked around for the next batch, I wondered how the trees in that cryptic message would be interlocked, or whether the pair still stood. With that in mind, I looked down, searching for two tree stumps close together, yet the thick foliage made it difficult to see through to the forest floor.

Rhonda appeared to be moving faster than I was, despite her high heels, and was almost out of sight. Myrtle was slowly trampling towards the next grouping of trees in her appointed direction, but they seemed to be spaced out fairly widely.

Before I could turn to track Julie's progress, my goddaughter yelled out, "I think I found something!"

I doubled back as fast as I could, but not too fast to twist an ankle. She was quite a ways off of the main trail, in a section of woods dotted with crumbling pieces of bunker.

By the time I reached the others, Julie had pushed back several lower branches of the tree she was standing next to, revealing a second trunk, wrapping around the first. The two had obviously been growing more entwined with every season, and in some spots it was almost impossible to tell which trunk belonged to which tree.

"Well done, Julie," I said as I reached them. "This certainly looks like the right pair of trees. I haven't seen any others that were so entangled as this pair. What about you two?" I looked to Rhonda and Myrtle, in case they had also found a pair of interlocked tree trunks.

"Nope, nothing like this," Myrtle confirmed.

"Me, either. I think Julie's found it," Rhonda said, her voice filled with motherly pride.

Her daughter pointed to a spot on the ground close to where the trees' trunks disappeared under the soil. "And look, there are tree roots sticking up out of the ground everywhere, except for there." She scraped the edge of her boot along the forest floor, revealing a stroke of sand but no roots. "See? It stands out. I think this might be the entrance to an underground bunker."

I studied the terrain, taking in all that she had mentioned, as well as the nearby location of two sections of crumbling bunker wall. "Well done, Julie. This sure does look and feel right. Let's dig in and see what we find."

I used the foldup shovel to scrape across the topsoil, then picked a random spot and dug down, again surprised at how easily the earth gave way. Sure, the soil was sandy and off of the main trail, so it wouldn't have been trampled on as much as the rest. But if this bunker's entrance had been hidden away for so long, I'd have expected the ground to be rock hard. *Just like the box under Atlas's collar*, I thought. It gave me a bad feeling about this whole situation, but I knew the others didn't think it to be strange, so I didn't bother to mention it.

Myrtle found a thick branch filled with pine needles that she used as a broom, effectively sweeping away layers of topsoil and small twigs.

Julie took another approach. She grabbed a thick log and began pounding it onto the ground in the spots Myrtle had cleared, seemingly with all of her might.

I looked at her curiously. "What are you doing?"

"If we're searching for the entrance to a bunker, I'm guessing it would be metal. If it's not buried too deep, I'm hoping it will make some sort of noise when I hit it with this stick."

I regarded my goddaughter, against surprised by how ingenious she was. "You're one smart cookie, Julie. I'll stop digging deep and start scraping off more of the topsoil."

"What should I do?" Rhonda asked.

"Be on the lookout, I guess. I doubt the park rangers will be happy to see us digging around back here."

"Smart thinking. I'll move a little closer to the main trail."

While Rhonda took a few steps to the right, the three of us continued digging, sweeping, and pounding. After the seventh thump, Julie struck gold when a dull clank greeted us. Her face lit up. "Bingo."

I sucked in my breath, hoping she was right. "Let's take a look."

Using my shovel, I pushed the dirt aside until I hit metal. Myrtle swept off as much topsoil as she could, as I scraped out the edges of what appeared to be an entrance, approximately four feet wide and two feet deep. A few minutes later and we had cleared the sand off of a metal door. It was red with oxidation and rust, but still quite solid. A large keyhole stuck up slightly on one side. Myrtle leaned down and blew sand out of the lock.

"I think we found it!" Rhonda exclaimed.

"It sure looks like it. I mean, this must be an entrance to the underground bunker."

There was only one problem remaining—the thickness of the door and the lock keeping trespassers out. "If that is a WWII bunker, the door is probably several inches thick of sold metal," Julie said, her voice full of wonder.

"Well, it's a good thing we have a key to try. Let's just hope that it opens this door." Myrtle looked over at me.

I glared at the door, that feeling of uneasiness returning. We'd caught Theresa after she'd stolen the box from my room, and we had gotten the jump on Anton when he tried following us here. But what if there were others searching for the missing art, as well? Had they gotten this far, realized they'd need the key to open the door, and were now watching us fumble around, waiting for the right moment to rob us?

The key burned a hole in my pocket. As much as I wanted to open the door, I was also terrified that we would be walking into a trap laid by whoever killed Jan. Yet I knew we had no choice but to see what was inside. Until we did, the police were not going to lend their assistance.

"Carmen, where's the key?"

"In my pocket."

Myrtle held out her hand.

I took the key out of my pocket, eyeing the long and heavy metal key in the palm of my hand. I stared at it for far too long, simultaneously scared and excited to see what was on the other side, before handing it over. "Here you go."

She turned to face us all, a grin splitting her face. "Okay, ladies, shall we find out if this key fits?"

28

Going Underground

I couldn't shake the feeling that someone was watching us as I handed the key over. It took Myrtle a few tries before the lock finally gave way. After I heard a sharp click, I grabbed ahold of the handle and pulled up. The metal door was heavier than I had anticipated, and I felt a tug in my shoulders as it groaned open.

I stared down at a metal ladder descending into a pitch-black hole. With my telephone flashlight, I could make out a single wooden crate on the floor, in the middle of the space.

"Is that it?" I moaned.

"What do you see?" Myrtle muttered as she pushed me aside and used her own phone to peer down into the darkened space. "I only see one crate. Where's the rest?"

"Maybe this isn't the final location. The crate might simply contain the next clue," Julie said, tempering our expectations.

"We might as well go down there and see what's inside. Carmen, why don't you go first," Myrtle said as she stepped away from the ladder, giving me room to climb down.

"Thanks," I muttered, before I crouched down and listened, as I cast my flashlight around the space. Luckily I didn't hear any scurrying noises, so there were no rodents to contend with. The ceiling also seemed to be intact, as in there were no gaping holes in it. I kicked the top two rungs of the ladder with my heel, but neither bent or broke free.

"Okay, I'm going down." I turned, positioning my body to step down into the hole, when my bestie rushed forward.

"Wait a second—now that we know there's something down there, we should call the local police. That's what we agreed to do, remember?"

Myrtle snorted. "No, we agreed to call them if we found the art. And that's still a big if. For all we know, there's another clue down there, not a painting."

When Myrtle stood behind me, as if waiting to go down the ladder, Rhonda held her hands up high, as if to try to stop us. "Before you go down there, let's take a moment and think this through. Someone killed Jan, presumably to find whatever is in that crate. As long as they don't have the key, they won't be able to get to it. But once we take it out of there, we may become the targets. I say we get this key to the proper authorities as quickly as we can. Now that we know there's something down there, the police will have to take action."

"I disagree," Myrtle said, her tone resolute. "I think we should search the bunker and see whether the crate contains the artwork, before we call anybody. If we get the local cops out here and it turns out to be another clue inside of that box, they may think we were intentionally wasting their precious time and not react later, when we may need their help. You know, that whole 'boy who cried wolf' scenario." Myrtle was quite convincing, even to me, and I knew that she was lying through her teeth.

However, both of us knew better than to blab about her true reason for wanting to search through that crate. Rhonda still didn't know that either one of us worked for the Rosewood Agency, which meant Myrtle couldn't explain why she wanted to go through the box now. Once the police took possession of it, she'd have to go through a lot of red tape before she would know what was inside and whether it was something our employer had been looking for.

Rhonda shivered. "I don't know, Myrtle. I have a bad feeling about this one. I think we should leave and call the cops in."

"I agree with Rhonda. If she feels uncomfortable, we should stop," I said.

But Myrtle wasn't having it. "Give me a break, Carmen! You've never hesitated in the past. So why now?"

"Because whoever killed Jan is probably looking for the missing art, just like we are. And I'm not convinced it was Anton or Theresa, so the murderer is probably still running around loose. And for all we know, they have already figured out that we have the key they need and are lying in ambush, waiting for us to bring the crate to the surface. We shouldn't dillydally, but get this straight to the police."

The high pitch of Myrtle's chortle caused several pigeons to take flight, despite the rain. It took her a moment to stop laughing before she finally answered. "Oh, please, stop being so dramatic. We've come all this way, and I'm not leaving until I know what's inside that crate. You can wait here if you want."

She slithered past me and Rhonda and down the ladder before any of us could stop her.

I pulled out my phone to call the cops, until I heard Myrtle's wolf whistle. "Isn't she a beauty?"

My finger hovered over the detective's name, but the familiar rush of adrenaline caused me to instead call out, "What did you find?"

"Come on down, if you want to know. Bring your shovel, too."

After a moment's hesitation, curiosity overwon the concerns for our safety.

As I stepped onto the ladder, I felt a rush of adrenaline coursing through my veins. What was inside that crate? I was about to find out.

I sprung off the last step and onto the solid floor. The temperature was surprisingly mild, which was a good thing, if there were paintings inside the crate. I shined my flashlight around and checked the walls and ceiling for damage. Everything looked to be intact and solid, albeit moldy.

"It looks safe enough for you to come down, if you two want to."

"Tell us what's inside the box first!" Rhonda called down.

I looked to the crate, still unopened. "Seriously, Myrtle?"

She shrugged. "I couldn't get it open on my own."

I shook my head as I used the foldup shovel as a crowbar and pried the crate's lid off.

Myrtle emitted a low whistle when I removed the plank and revealed a trio of paintings inside. "Would you look at that?"

"What have you found?" Julie cried out.

"Three paintings—come down here if you want to see them!" Myrtle yelled back.

I pulled the first painting out of the crate and shined my flashlight on it. It was a gorgeous impressionistic rendering of a sunset over the sea. I couldn't discern that artist's name in the low light, but I could tell that it was exquisite. Based on the coloring and brushstrokes, I guessed that it was by Claude Monet.

Julie and Rhonda arrived in time to see me remove painting number two from the crate, an abstract portrait of a young girl. In the background, a tiny man with curly hair floated above her, playing a violin. "Oh, my, that looks like a Marc Chagall!"

The third artist's identity was more obvious, thanks to the subject's cubistic portrayal. Rhonda shined her phone's flashlight onto the canvas. "I don't recognize the model, and the brushstrokes are much looser than his typical work, but that has got to be by Pablo Picasso. This must be a study he'd made, as part of a larger work."

Rhonda took her time examining all three with her flashlight before giving us her professional opinion. "These all appear to be in good condition, which is a miracle given the circumstances. All three are pretty small and none are what I would call the artists' best work, but they are still worth quite a bit. Based on their names alone, I'd estimate that these three are worth upwards of twenty-five million dollars on today's market. Maybe more, if a few hardcore collectors get into a bidding war over them."

I couldn't keep my eyes off of the paintings. Rhonda was right in that none were masterpieces, but all were fine examples of the artists' works. "I can imagine the story behind their discovery might add a few hundred thousand more to the price."

Rhonda laughed. "That's true."

"Now that we know what's inside, can you call the lead investigator handing Rhonda's case for us, Carmen?" Julie asked. "Tell him about this and ask if he has a local contact he trusts. We need to get the police involved before

Jan's murderer catches up with us."

"Sure thing." I dialed as requested, but nothing happened. "Shoot, there's no signal down here. Tell you what, why don't we take the crate with us, and call him from the van?"

"That sounds like a good plan," Julie agreed.

The sound of a gun's barrel being cocked made me freeze. A male voice boomed down the ladder. "No, I think I'll take that crate, instead."

29

Treasure Found

My grip on my phone tightened. "Who's there?"

"Surprise." When I looked up to see Joris the cameraman with an old revolver in his hand, a sigh escaped my lips. I should have known he would also be after the missing art, as soon as Anton the director said that any WWII buff would have known about the codes.

"Carmen, you were right!" Rhonda cried.

Joris rushed down the ladder before any of us could react. "If you do what I ask, I'll leave you alone. But don't test me."

I eyed his weapon skeptically. It looked to be an old Luger P08, a German handgun used during WWII that had been a sought-after souvenir by the American troops. These days, they were worth a pretty penny because they were fairly rare. "Come on, do you expect us to believe that your relic still works?"

"This Luger P08 may be old, but I keep my weapons clean and in working condition. In fact, I tested this one last week, and it sighted perfectly."

I considered testing his theory, but figured it wasn't worth dying to do so. "What do you want?"

"Whatever is in that crate. Dad told me all about the Klavers and their use of codes to relay the bunker's location to its owner, as well as the rumors that there were still a few crates hidden away."

Rhonda whimpered.

"I have no interested in hurting any of you, unless you provoke me." He motioned us to one side of the space with his gun, ensuring our compliance.

"You knew all along that the scarf was encoded, didn't you? Knitted codes were commonplace in WWII; a buff like you would have known that."

His lopsided grin emanated pride. "Sure did. It was sheer luck that brought Jan onto Rhonda's show. He had no idea of what he had in his possession. There he was, crying and moping about that worthless scarf. If he only knew! After I messed with my camera's feed so that Anton would dismiss me, it was easy to short out the power and take the scarf from him."

"Then why did you kill him?"

Joris jutted his chin up. "I didn't mean to, but when I tried to lock him in the closet, he fought back. If he hadn't resisted, I wouldn't have had to push him so hard. It's not my fault he hit his head on that desk. Trust me, it would have been much simpler if he'd lived. The scarf was easy enough to hide under my jacket, but the box was more of a challenge. If he had just gotten into that closet, I could have taken the box, as well, and slipped away before anyone found him. But when I saw all that blood pouring out of his head, I knew the police would be called in, and I didn't want to be arrested for murder. So I chose to wait them out and come back for the box after the police left. But Carmen beat me to it."

He gazed over at me. "I saw you slip it into Rhonda's bag. I figured it held more secrets, but I didn't realize it was a key to opening this bunker."

He held out his hand. "I'll take that key now."

Part of me wanted to toss it in the corner and make a break for it, but I knew all four of us wouldn't be able to climb up fast enough, especially considering Joris was prepared to shoot. So I tossed it at his feet, within easy reach.

"How did you find us? Did you put a tracker on my phone?" I badgered him in the hopes of slowing him down, worried that he would regard us to be nuisances he would rather be rid of, after he'd opened the crate.

"Once I realized I needed this key, I figured it was in the box you'd taken. I went to your hotel to retrieve it, but when I pulled up, I saw you all getting into a van and driving away from the hotel."

I felt like such an amateur again. But his words made me realize that my premonitions earlier were not completely off-base. "Wait—so you had already followed the trail? That was why the soil was loose—you had already dug up the marker at Westerstraete. And here, too. You'd already found the door, hadn't you? I knew it felt off. See, ladies, I'm not crazy!"

Yet the trio only grimaced at me, their eyes still trained on Joris's gun.

Our captor dipped his head. "Yes, I had. It didn't take me long to decipher the scarf's message or find the Westerstraete estate, and I drove down south as soon as the police released us. Once I found this bunker's entrance and realized I needed the key, I figured it was in the box. Otherwise I wouldn't have had to return to Amsterdam. But it was a nice coincidence to see that you were heading in the direction of Hazelbroek. I figured it was only a matter of time before you found the bunker and brought me the key."

Myrtle turned to me. "I'm sorry, Carmen, I didn't see him tailing me."

"It's okay, Myrtle. You spotted Anton."

Joris began to laugh. "Anton was following you, too? I should have figured he would have. He kept blathering on about needing to find a new subject for a documentary."

"Why are you doing this?" I asked.

"The artwork that Jan's granddad hid away is a legend among WWII buffs. My granddad was fascinated with the Klavers and talked a lot about what might be in the missing crates. He always figured it would be a collection of Old Masters work worth millions." Joris looked longingly at the crate. "Let's find out if my grandfather was right."

He motioned for us to move to the far side of the space, away from the ladder.

Only then did he open the lid and look inside. His expression betrayed his confusion. "Are there only three paintings hidden away in here?"

I couldn't help but laugh. Joris sneered at me, then pulled the first painting out, gasping as he did. Once he'd examined all three, he turned to me with an extremely satisfied smirk. "There aren't many, but they are all valuable. Granddad would have been proud of me for finding them. Which means I'll be taking this crate with me."

"The art should go to the rightful owner!" I cried.

Joris jutted up his chin. "Granddad figured whoever found it had as much right to it as the legal owner's heirs. It had been hidden away for decades, meaning they weren't even alive when the art was stolen."

He pushed the lid down and lifted the crate up, weighing it with one hand, a frown on his face as he did.

I understood his dilemma. The crate wasn't heavy, but it was bulky and if he carried it up the ladder, he would not be able to keep his gun trained on us, leaving him exposed. And if he was silly enough to do that, I would most certainly wrestle him off of the ladder.

He nodded at my bestie. "Miss Rhodes, would you do the honors of placing this crate at the top of the stairs? Climb up and then I'll hand it to you. Don't try calling out or running away, otherwise your friends will pay the price."

He pointed the gun at the rest of us, to make his point clear.

Rhonda stumbled forward, tears dotting her cheeks, but did as he asked. However, the rain streaming through the opening made the ladder so slippery she had trouble climbing up. Once she reached the top, he handed her the box. Rhonda set the crate on the ground and climbed back down without more than a whimper.

After she'd rejoined us, she grabbed Julie's hand tight.

"What are you going to do to us?" I asked, my voice breaking as I did.

"I'm not going to hurt you, if that's what you mean. At least, as long as you remain standing against that wall until I get out."

Joris backed up to the ladder, his gun pointed at us the whole time. When he pocketed it to climb through the opening, I had a horrible sense of foreboding.

Once he reached the top, he looked down through the hole. "I'm a man of my word, so I won't harm you. But I can't have you following me, either."

He swung the heavy door closed, and the space went pitch black. Seconds later, we heard the scratch of a key turning as he locked us in.

30

Confession Time

"We are all going to die!" Rhonda cried.

"No, that's not true. The bunker is large, we won't suffocate right away," I reasoned and switched on my phone's flashlight.

"We'll more likely die from dehydration or starvation, if someone doesn't find us soon," Myrtle added, and turned her phone's light on, too.

Rhonda's wails only increased.

"Way to go, Myrtle," I hissed at her as I moved in to comfort Rhonda. But Julie got there first and wrapped a protective arm around her mother's shoulders.

"Stop it, you two. Mom, we are not going to die down here. We just have to wait for someone to find us, that's all."

"But no one is looking!"

"Cindy is, or will be as soon as she can't reach you on the phone; of that I'm certain. You're supposed to be taping tomorrow, right?" My voice was full of confidence, but the truth was, Rhonda was right. Cindy would scour the ends of the earth to find her show's star, once she discovered that Rhonda was unreachable. Yet no one knew we were missing, and even if they did, no one would know where to look.

The only person, other than Joris, that we'd run into since we'd arrived in Hazelbroek was Anton, and I'd taken his car keys to ensure he didn't continue to follow us.

CONFESSION TIME

"Anyone have a pickpocket set?" Myrtle grumbled.

I shook my head. "I don't think that would do us any good. It's not an easy lock to pick. The metal is so thick, it'll take dynamite or a serious welding torch to get it open. At least, without the key."

When Rhonda began to tear up again, I added, "But this rainstorm can't last all day. There will be more joggers and dog walkers soon, I promise." I felt terrible for getting the others into this predicament.

"What about your partner, Sophie? Can she get us out of this mess?" Rhonda's voice had a strangely high pitch. I knew there was still tension between the two, but this seemed like the wrong time to get upset about the Baroness's aloof behavior.

"I'm afraid not. Lady Sophie doesn't know where we're at. As far as I know, she's still in Switzerland comforting Princess Alexandria."

Rhonda snorted. "Lady, my foot."

"Excuse me? What has gotten into you?" I pointed my phone's flashlight at her, shocked to see how riled up Rhonda was getting. I knew they'd had their differences but had thought they'd come to a truce. In fact, Rhonda had even mentioned that she was going to research the Baroness's tiara's origins, as a way of trying to impress her.

Rhonda grabbed my hand. "It's Sophie—she's not who she says she is."

I pulled back and stared at her. "What are you saying?"

"I don't know who Sophie really is, but she can't be the Baroness Rutherford of Roxburghshire, as she claims. I researched the tiara and found out that it's a famous piece that was commissioned for the Rutherford family around two hundred years ago. But that line died out two generations ago. Sophie can't be a Rutherford, at least not a legitimate one."

I shook my head, refusing to believe her. "That can't be right. It must be a mistake."

"Nope, my research is crystal clear. The last Rutherford died in 1913, without leaving a wife or child behind. There is no mention of where his possessions ended up, but it appears that most of his things were sold to pay off his many debts. Which means someone in Sophie's family probably bought it, somewhere along the line. But purchasing a tiara doesn't mean you get to use the title. I suppose Sophie could be the descendant of one of the last baron's illegitimate children, or she's lying about her heritage completely. Either way, she has clearly not told you the truth about her family."

"It's not possible. She couldn't have been lying to me this whole time…" My voice trailed off as I thought back on the intense vetting process the Rosewood Agency used on its employees. Under such intense scrutiny, I couldn't believe that Reggie's team hadn't discovered Sophie's true identity. Yet if he knew she was lying, why had he hired her? I looked to my company contact, wondering whether she and Reggie were in on whatever scam the Baroness was trying to pull.

Yet when I looked to Myrtle, she appeared to be as shocked as I felt. "I can't believe it either. I don't mean to doubt you, Rhonda, but are you certain?"

"One hundred percent."

Myrtle wrung her hands together. "But why would she lie like that?"

I thought about my partner, so at ease with her royal friends. "I don't know, but I'm going to find out the next time I see her. But could you give me the chance to talk to her about this privately before you say anything about your findings? I don't doubt your research, but I would hate to embarrass her unnecessarily. There must be a reasonable explanation. Can you forget about it for now, and just treat her like the baroness she at least claims to be?"

Rhonda gulped and gave me a sidelong glance. "I'll do my best. I just hate it when people lie to me."

I laid a hand on her shoulder, ignoring the wave of guilt rising up inside of me at having lied to her for years. "That's all I can ask."

When I looked up, Julie's head was bowed over, as if she had a heavy burden on her shoulders. "Mom, I have a confession to make. I haven't worked for the American Embassy for months—I work for Interpol now. Dave Swanson, the agent you met in Luxembourg, is my partner. I was with him at that auction in Luxembourg, until you and Aunt Carmen showed up."

"What are you saying—that you've been lying to me all this time?"

"I guess I have. But I didn't do it to hurt you, but to keep you from worrying about me."

"I don't understand. How can someone I love deceive me like that—and so easily?" Rhonda's confusion made me gulp. Here I was, her best friend, and I'd been lying to her about my work and lifestyle for almost two decades.

"It was never my intention! My boss at the embassy knew I wasn't happy and thought I would be a good fit for the art recovery team at Interpol. It turns out, he was right. I was planning on telling you, once I was certain that it is the right job for me. I guess I just hadn't figured out how to do so."

Rhonda sat up straight. "Wait—art recovery? I thought you disliked your art history classes. That was why you switched to international relations, isn't it?"

Julie looked uncomfortable. "I guess I didn't tell you the whole truth about that, either. I didn't switch to international relations; I majored in both that and art history. You gave me so much flak for doing too much during college, and I didn't want you to dissuade me from doing both degrees. So I fibbed a little. It didn't really feel like a lie at the time."

Rhonda narrowed her eyes at her daughter. "Huh. I see."

Yet when Julie took her hand, Rhonda looked up at her daughter shyly, as if she was seeing her for the first time. "I know we are as opposite as can be, but I do love you, Julie, and I'll support you in whatever you do. But please, don't lie to me anymore. I can't take it." Rhonda wrapped her arms around her daughter before she could reply.

The lump in my throat wasn't just my emotional response to the sight before me. I knew I was going to have to tell Rhonda about my work as an art sleuth, but now was not the time to do so.

Myrtle nodded towards the ladder. "What do you say we do now, Carmen?"

Watching my friend embrace her daughter so tightly made my throat stick. I felt responsible for pushing them to follow this trail, which meant it was on me to get us out of this, alive.

"It's too bad we can't hear if the rain has stopped or not, but I'm tired of waiting around and doing nothing."

I climbed up the ladder and used the foldup shovel to pound on the metal door. The clanging sound was so loud, it hurt my ears, but I kept at it.

After several minutes, Myrtle pulled on my pant leg. "Stop making that racket! You're giving me a headache. It must still be raining. We can always try again later."

"We're so far off the trail, I doubt anyone will hear us, anyway," Rhonda moaned.

Her words made me raise my shovel again. "I refuse to give up. If we don't do something, then we'll never get rescued."

Before the metal could make contact again, a muffled cry reached my ears.

"Over here! I think I hear them!"

31

Unexpected Savior

I pounded that shovel as hard as I could so the person could pinpoint our location, screaming as I did. After three hits, I waited and listened again.

"Rhonda Rhodes? Carmen De Luca? Can you hear me?" the same male voice shouted again. Sure enough, he was getting closer. I hit the door once more for good measure, just before I heard the man yell out, "Look—there's a door. They must be down there."

Now that he was above us, his voice seemed familiar. "Anton? Is that you?"

"Yes, it is," he yelled back. "Carmen, is Rhonda with you?"

"Yes, and Myrtle and Julie. Are you by yourself? Joris the cameraman took the key to the bunker door."

"I'm with the local police. Let me get them over here, and then we'll figure out how to get you out."

For a split second, I wondered whether this was another trap, but seconds later I heard Anton yelling for the police. Soon, several voices were conferring overhead, but now in Dutch.

A few seconds later, Anton yelled back down at us. "The fire department should be able to cut through the door, but it's going to take them a few minutes to get their trucks and equipment out here. Can you step away from the opening, until they've finished?"

"Sure thing."

There was a ruckus up above, and then Anton yelled down again. "They are going to try to cut through it now. Step as far away from the door as you can, okay?"

"Will do!" I screamed up. We pushed ourselves against the back wall, and soon the screech of metal on metal filled the air. The noise was horrifically loud, but soon a shower of sparks rained down the ladder, meaning they'd made it through the thick metal. I pushed my fingers deeper into my ears, praying the saw would cut faster.

Soon enough, the firemen were pulling the door free, and real rain coursed down through the hole. I breathed in deeply, greatly relieved to smell fresh air again.

I looked up to see Anton smiling down at us. Boy, was I glad to see him. Behind him were a few uniformed officers.

"Do you need help getting up?" he called down.

"No, we've got this."

I helped my bestie, her daughter, and my company contact up the ladder, before climbing up.

All three were screaming for the police to find Joris, that he had stolen the missing artwork and locked them into the bunker. It saved us all time, and gave me hope that the cops might just find him, while he still had the paintings in his possession.

Once I reached the top, I joined Anton under his umbrella, then held out my hand to him. "Thank you for rescuing us. But how did you know where to find us? Did you have a tracker on our rental car, after all?"

He grinned at me. "No, nothing that fancy. After you took my keys, I had to call a locksmith to get back into my car. Luckily, she was quite fast and as soon as she was done, I drove around looking for your van. I just had to know what you would find at the end of the trail. After I spotted your van in the parking lot, I noticed Joris's Toyota parked close by. Before I could step out, he'd run back to his car with a crate in his hand and sped off. I thought about following him, but I had a bad feeling that he may have done something to you."

"What do you mean?"

"I knew Joris was a WWII buff and recalled that he'd gotten quite excited about Jan's puzzle box during the first show and had asked to take a closer look at it. So when I saw his car here, I got suspicious. The police had released Rene, so I knew Jan's killer was still on the loose. For all I knew, it could have been Joris. And it sounds like I was right."

"Well done," I mumbled.

"I walked along the main trail, calling out your names, but when I couldn't find you in the park, I was convinced he'd harmed you. That's when I called the local police. They weren't too interested, until I mentioned that Rhonda Rhodes was one of the people I was searching for. Then they agreed to help. Apparently Cindy had already submitted a missing persons report."

I couldn't help but chuckle. "Good old Cindy, I knew she'd come through."

"I suppose that's one advantage to being famous. Thanks for following us," Rhonda said.

I blushed. "Sorry about your keys, Anton. I really didn't know who to trust. Apparently we chose the wrong person to take into our confidence."

He shrugged, but kept his eyes on me. "How could you have known? I'm just glad I did find you. Who knows how long it would have taken, otherwise."

"You're right. It was only a couple of hours, but it felt like a lifetime. How can we ever repay you?"

The twinkle in his eye told me he was hoping I would ask that. "What do you say to letting me interview you for my documentary?"

"Aha, so you are going to go through with that?"

"You bet! Especially now that you have found the art. Where is it? I haven't seen the police remove anything from the bunker."

"It was just that one crate. Joris took it, then locked us in. I have no idea where he was headed."

Anton's face fell for a moment, then lit up again. "A police chase will only help with the marketing. I'm sure they'll catch Joris, in the end."

Something behind me caught his attention, and he nodded to whatever it was, over my shoulder. "I think that officer is trying to get your attention."

I turned around to see several officers huddled under the Green Cathedral, along with Myrtle, Rhonda, and Julie. A young policeman was waving for me to join them.

I turned to Anton. "I guess he doesn't want to get wet. Shall we?"

32

Bloody Fingerprint

It took me several minutes to recount all that had happened since Jan's murder yesterday afternoon. The detective listened silently while I explained how we had decoded the scarf, confronted and interrogated Anton in Hazelbroek, and finally found the artwork in the bunker, only to have Joris steal it and then lock us in.

I wasn't certain he believed me until he asked whether I could recall the titles and artists' names of the paintings in the crate. I quickly wrote them down for the officer, glad he'd decided to take my statement seriously.

After we'd all relayed our ordeal in detail to the lead detective, Rhonda, Myrtle, Julie, and I were driven over to the hospital for a checkup. On the ride over, I texted the titles to Reggie, then checked my messages. All of our phones had gone off in a chaotic chorus as soon as we were above ground again, but the officers demanded that we refrain from contacting the outside world until we'd given them our statements. Several missed calls were from Cindy, I noted with surprise. She must have called me, when she couldn't reach Rhonda, and most likely before she'd submitted that missing persons report, I realized.

I looked back at my friend and her daughter, sitting two rows behind me in the police's spacious van. Considering Rhonda had her arms wrapped tight around Julie and her eyes shut, I decided to call Cindy back myself.

"Carmen, thank goodness. I haven't been able to reach Rhonda for hours.

Is she with you? And is she alright?"

I didn't balk at her lack of concern for me, knowing that Rhonda's well-being was paramount. She was the star of *Antiques Time*, after all.

"Yes and yes. We're on our way to the hospital now."

"Why—has she been injured?"

"None of us are hurt, but Joris did lock us into that underground bunker, and the police want to have us checked out before releasing us."

Cindy was quiet a moment. "Carmen, are you pulling my leg? I had been calling you and Rhonda to let you know that the police found Joris's fingerprint in Jan's blood. But he's disappeared."

I cringed. "I know where he's not."

"What happened exactly? How did you end up in a bunker?"

"It's a long story, but the short version is we found a code hidden in the scarf and decoded it. It led us to an underground bunker in the southern Netherlands where we found the artwork Jan's grandfather had hidden away. But Joris followed us, took the art, and locked us in the bunker about three hours ago. The police and fire department just freed us, and now we're on our way to the hospital."

"Oh my—that's incredible! I can't wait to hear the long version. We'll have to feature the artwork you found on the show."

"I suppose you can, once the police find it again. Joris took it after he locked us in, and they haven't found him yet. I have to have faith that the police will find him, eventually."

"Now that they want him for Jan's murder, as well as theft, I'm certain they'll find him. Is Rhonda really okay?"

The concern in her voice made clear that my word was not enough to satisfy her. "She's fine. Do you want to talk to her?"

I could hear Cindy sigh in relief. "Yes, please."

I held my phone out to Rhonda, still entangled with her daughter. "It's Cindy. She's really worried about you."

Rhonda leaned over the seat and grabbed my phone. "Oh, Cindy! I'm fine, really I am. Thanks to Carmen, Julie, and Myrtle."

33

Tiaras and Titles

After a quick checkup, we were all released and headed back to our hotel. To my surprise, the Baroness was in the lobby, waiting for me. "Lady Sophie! What are you doing here?"

She rose slowly, steadying herself with her cane before approaching. "It sounds like I missed out on another exciting adventure. I heard you were involved in a treasure hunt gone wrong. Reggie and I were worried about you and Myrtle, so I flew back the moment I got word."

"On the princess's jet, I assume."

"Naturally."

Rhonda sniggered behind me, making me whip around to face her, giving her the most stern expression I could muster.

"Hello, Sophie," she murmured as she waved at my partner.

Myrtle pushed forward around us and slapped my partner lightly on the shoulder. "It was good of you to fly over. We're fine—even the doctors agree, otherwise they wouldn't have released us."

"Hi, Sophie. If you don't mind, we're pretty beat. Mom and I are going to head up to our room. We'll see you all later." Julie pulled her mother forward by the hand. But when she looked back at me with a knowing look on her face, I did wonder how much Rhonda had already told her about Sophie's tiara. Considering Julie had omitted Sophie's title, I suspected my bestie had told her everything.

Only after they were gone did my partner ask, "What happened exactly? Why were you hospitalized?"

"You'd better sit back down, it's a long story," Myrtle said.

After Myrtle and I caught her up to speed, Sophie leaned forward to grasp my hand, squeezing it gently. "That's incredible. I don't know who the magnet for trouble is—you or Rhonda. But I'm glad that it ended well."

"It is a tossup," I admitted, then looked over at Myrtle. "Would you mind if I had a few minutes alone with my partner?"

"Sure thing. I'll catch up with you later." Myrtle rose too quickly and sped off, leaving us alone in the hotel lobby.

After Myrtle was out of hearing range, Sophie looked at me with one eyebrow raised. "What's going on?"

I had trouble meeting her eye. She had been my favorite partner for many years. We had relied on each other to get out of some hairy situations, and she had even gotten injured while saving my life. I thought I knew her through and through. But it turned out, I didn't really know her at all. At least, not if Rhonda's research into the tiara turned out to be true. Asking Sophie about it now meant having to face that fact, and I just wasn't certain I was ready to do so. But I couldn't let it go, either.

"Earth to Carmen. Based on your pensive expression and how quickly Myrtle departed, I have the strong feeling that I'm missing something. And it didn't escape my attention that neither Rhonda or Julie used my title when addressing me. Would you care to enlighten me?"

"How is Princess Alexandria coping?"

My partner's eyes rolled to the ceiling. "She's alright, I suppose, but still nervous around her staff. It's difficult for her to go forward, knowing that those closest to her were lying to her the entire time."

The irony of her comment caused me to snort. "Speaking of which, Sophie, I don't know how to ask this politely, so I'm going to be direct about it. Rhonda and her expert friend have researched your tiara's provenance."

I locked eyes with her, expecting some sort of shocked reaction. But all she did was look vaguely amused. "Oh? That's quite lovely actually. I recall she'd mentioned knowing an expert she could ask, but I hadn't expected her to actually reach out to her."

I smiled. "Then you don't know Rhonda that well. I knew the moment she asked you about it that she would make a point of doing so."

"What did she discover?"

Sophie's voice and expression held no trepidation. She really didn't seem to know what I was about to say. "That the tiara had been commissioned by the Rutherford family in Roxburghshire two hundred years ago. When she traced the line, Rhonda discovered that the last Baron Rutherford of Roxburghshire died in 1913, unmarried and childless. Which means, according to her research, you can't be the legitimate heir to the title."

Man, it hurt saying those words aloud. It didn't help that Sophie looked as if I had slapped her in the face. For a split second, I felt like a complete fool for even asking her about this, until I noticed that she seemed more scared than angry.

"Wait—is it true? Have you been lying about being a baroness? I have to know."

"Yes," was her strangled reply.

I recoiled from her, suddenly disgusted by her presence. "Who are you?"

Sophie's forehead creased as she looked up at me with watery eyes. "The same Sophie you've always known."

"No, the Lady Sophie I know is a direct descendant of a titled family."

My partner sighed softly. "My paternal grandfather was a proud Scotsman, and quite a successful gambler. He managed to win country estates, racehorses, and even a tiara bought at an estate sale, one that had belonged to a titled family from a minor house of no importance." She tapped the tiara nestled in her French bun.

My eyes widened as I took in the implications of her words. "Your granddad was quite the gambler."

"Yes, well, that's what he always claimed. When he discovered that this tiara had been owned by the Baron of Roxburghshire, and that his line had died out, Granddad decided to adopt the title as his own. He enjoyed playing the part, and my grandmother loved being a baroness."

Sophie paused a moment, her mouth turning up, presumably at a memory.

"Grandmama even insisted their staff call them 'lady' and 'lord,' even though most of them knew it was a ruse. My own mother didn't know we were not really royalty until she turned twenty-one. For better or worse, Mother kept the family tradition going by only telling me the truth when I reached that age, as well."

When she looked away again, I could feel my anger dissolving. It sounded like she hadn't chosen to lie about her title, but had only perpetuated the lie her family had created many years ago.

"So you see, I was in a conundrum when I found out. I had been raised as a baroness and saw my title as an integral part of my identity. My friends and social network saw me as Lady Sophie Rutherford of Roxburghshire, and no one really cared further."

"But why did Reggie let it slide? Or did you not tell him?"

"I had decided to keep it from him, but Reggie did an exhaustive background check and discovered the truth eventually. At first, he would not hire me, because of it. It took a lot of convincing before Reggie would let me on the team. But I play the part well—I was born into it, after all, and I know the right people. And my title enabled me to use my connections to get agents like you into parties you wouldn't be admitted to, otherwise. When he finally relented, he did so on the condition that I promised to keep my secret from everyone—even Myrtle—and I gladly agreed."

"But why would you want to work for the Rosewood Agency? You don't need the money."

She chuckled. "That's true, I do not. To this day, some family members believe that my grandfather either cheated at cards or lied about how he acquired certain possessions. I don't know if the insinuations are merely irritating rumors that certain cousins love to bring up during family gatherings, or the truth. It hadn't mattered to me, not until my husband's portrait was stolen from our home shortly after he passed. It was the first time I'd experienced what it was to have things taken from you, and it was not a fine feeling. Which is why I talked to Reggie about how I could help."

I looked at Sophie with new eyes, unsure as to how I should react.

When I remained silent, she asked in a shy voice, "What does this mean for us?"

I felt so confused. On the one hand, her family history shouldn't matter. I also knew not to take her deception personally as she had been lying to everyone, not just me—just as I lied to those I loved about my true profession for so many years. Yet she was always so hoity-toity and often treated others as if they were less than her. I figured her superiority complex was born out of her privileged background. And, in fact, it was. Yet that background was a lie. Knowing her truth made it seem as if she was a complete phony, and I didn't know how that made me feel. "I'm not certain. Give me a little time to process this, okay?"

"Of course; it's a lot to take in."

I started to rise, planning on returning to my room to let this all sink in, but she looked so forlorn, I couldn't leave her like this. "Are you heading back to Princess Alexandria's home in Switzerland?"

"She flew down to Lake Cuomo this morning and invited me to join her there. I told her about your adventures, and she said you are welcome to join us."

I was glad to hear there were no hard feelings between the princess and me. After Dave and I accused her of being a criminal mastermind, I figured she'd prefer not to see me again. Still, I didn't feel like sitting around with an elderly royal sipping tea and listening to her and Sophie gossiping about their snobby friends. "No, it's not really my scene. But you should go."

Sophie bit her lip. "What about you?"

"Rhonda and I are going to take a short trip to the French Riviera after she's finished filming her final show in Amsterdam."

"It is lovely this time of year."

Sophie looked away just as a tear started to roll down her cheek. "Is this how our European adventure ends?"

"I guess it is." Saying goodbye was suddenly far more difficult than I'd anticipated. We rarely socialized when we were back in the States. If I didn't return to work, this would most likely be the last time we saw each other. Despite her lying about her title, Sophie was a good person, underneath all that bling-bling.

"With a little luck, Reggie will find you another assignment. If you want to come back, that is."

It was painful to hear her say "you" instead of "us." "That is the million-dollar question. I honestly don't know what I want right now."

"Perhaps after a little downtime, you'll figure it out."

Sophie rose and extended a hand. I shook my head as I pulled her in for a hug. She allowed it, but I don't think she really enjoyed it.

Still, when I released her, she asked, "Could we have dinner tonight, to celebrate our successes during our European tour? It doesn't feel right, parting like this."

Her modest tone helped to soften my resolve to say goodbye now and be done with it. We had been partners for more than fifteen years; I could sit down to one more dinner with her, I figured.

"That sounds lovely. Why don't I invite Myrtle to join us? Rhonda and Julie would probably prefer to dine alone, anyway," I added quickly, saving us both face.

Sophie breathed a sigh of relief. "That sounds perfect."

34

Poorly Timed Ping

After Sophie went up to her room, I headed over to the hotel bar, suddenly in desperate need of a stiff drink and a little alone time. However, before I could take a sip of my margarita, Rhonda bounced into view.

"Carmen—there you are! Cindy just called to let me know that the German police picked Joris up for a busted taillight a half hour ago, and the crate of artwork was still in the trunk. Apparently he tried to deny having stolen the paintings because he must have figured that we were still locked up in the bunker. I bet this means the police will be able to return them to their rightful owner or their descendants, after all. At least, if they can find them."

"What a relief." I couldn't tell Rhonda that I had already texted the three paintings' titles to our employer. Seeing as tracking down lost artwork was the Rosewood Agency's thing, I expected our researchers to figure out who the rightful owner was, long before the police did. Once we had located them, we would share the intel with the men in uniform.

"Julie and I are going to meet up with Cindy for drinks so she can give us all the details. I'll call you later and fill you in, okay?" My bestie zipped away before I could reply. That was alright by me. I still hadn't wrapped my head around all that Sophie had shared, and now I had the ramifications of Joris's arrest and the return of the artwork to consider.

Before I could begin to process these turns of events, my phone let out a series of pings, alerting me to a new notification. My breath caught in my throat as I realized it was the tone I set to go off when there was news about Esmeralda Bianci. I opened the message, eager to read it. Dottoressa Esmerelda Bianci had died two days ago, and her funeral was being held in Florence this afternoon.

A surge of rage rose up from within. I had wanted to attend that funeral, in the hopes of learning more about my father and his family's history. Yet even a private jet couldn't get me there in time.

Against my better judgment, I downed half of my margarita, regretting it instantly. As I hung my head over the bar, feeling even more forlorn and confused than before I ordered my drink, my phone began to ring.

"What now?" I muttered. The number was unfamiliar to me. "This is Carmen De Luca."

"Good afternoon. I am Lorenzo Columbo, lawyer to Dottoressa Esmerelda Bianci—may she rest in peace."

I sat up a little straighter. The man's voice had a wonderful Italian lilt to it. "I just read about her death. The funeral is taking place today, isn't it?"

"Yes, in one hour. My final task is to distribute her possessions, in accordance with her last will and testament. She has a package that she insisted I send to you as soon as I received it. I can have it shipped overnight to you, anywhere in the world; all I need is your address."

"What exactly did she leave me?"

"I do not know. She sealed the package herself and instructed her chauffeur to bring it to me, after her passing. I have not opened it, out of respect for the Dottoressa."

The idea that it could be an explosive device briefly flitted through my head, but she had seemed to take a real shine to me, so I doubted it contained anything lethal. "Okay. I'm in Amsterdam for three more days. Can you send it to my hotel?"

"Certainly. It will be delivered within twenty-four hours."

After I relayed the hotel's address and we said goodbye, the bartender asked whether I wanted another drink. I declined, but stayed seated at the bar just a little longer, wondering what Bianci could have left me.

35

A Killer Inheritance

"Can you get it closed now?" Rhonda asked, as she rocked back and forth on top of her overly full luggage in an attempt to squish down its contents.

I tugged on the straps as hard as I dared, slightly worried I might tear the leather, until I finally got both closed. "Got it!"

"Phew. I guess I did go a little crazy during our shopping trip yesterday."

"A little? I think you bought pretty much every dress you came across that was in your size."

"True, but there are so many talented local designers here that you can't find in the States, I couldn't pass them up."

"They do look good on you," I admitted.

"They do, don't they?" She smiled as she twirled, showing off the great cut of her new babydoll-style dress.

"So, how does it feel to have the first set of tapings over and done with?"

"Wonderful! I hope for Cindy's sake the shows in Paris are less eventful. I don't know if her nerves can take another death or treasure hunt. Although the publicity from the police investigation definitely helped with the show's success."

"Are the crew already on their way, or do they have to pack up the set still?"

"As far as I know, everything is loaded up and ready to go. They'll have everything set up in Paris before the end of the week, which gives us five whole days of uninterrupted girl time." She giggled as she wrapped her arms around my neck. "Or is Dave going to join us?"

I grabbed ahold of her arms. "No, it's just you and me."

Rhonda and I were getting ready for our trip to the French Riviera, to celebrate the successful taping of her first three European shows, as well as surviving our ordeal with Joris. Julie had left the day before to go back to work. To my chagrin, she couldn't say what her next assignment entailed, or even whether she was working with Dave. Yet it was probably for the best that I didn't know what Dave was up to for the time being. My head was still a mess, and right now I didn't know what I wanted from my professional or personal life.

Myrtle was on her way to London to help with another case before flying home. However, she had only left Amsterdam after helping the police identify the owner of the artwork Jan's granddad had hidden away. Rosewood's researchers had found the family that had owned all three within hours of receiving my text.

Sophie was already in Italy, presumably lounging around in the sun with Princess Alexandria. Thankfully, Rhonda had agreed to leave her be. There was no reason to confront her, I argued, considering they wouldn't be working together again. After several talks with Myrtle and Reggie, I had finally managed to convince them that Rhonda was not agent material.

It was only after everyone had left Amsterdam and Rhonda had finished taping her final show that I dared to tell my bestie the truth about my job and Carlos's death, as well as my work-related troubles with Dave, my fruitless search for Antonio, and my discovery of Esmerelda Bianci and her cryptic connection to my father.

I wasn't certain how she would deal with me having lied to her for so long and about so much. But after taking a few minutes to let it all sink in, she wrapped me up in an all-forgiving hug, and that was that.

I believed that I had Julie's confession to thank for the ease with which Rhonda had accepted my deceit and moved on. I supposed I had done the same with Sophie, during our last meal together before she left for Italy.

Rhonda nodded to the package sticking out of my purse. "Are you going to open that or just keep carrying it around? It might be important, especially since your great-aunt insisted her lawyer send it to you so soon after her death."

I stared at the thick envelope, dreading opening it. I figured it had something to do with my father, and I wasn't certain I was emotionally ready to face the truth about his death, or his life. I hadn't even gotten the chance to meet him, seeing as he was killed before I was born, but the stories my mother told me about him made him out to be an incredibly loving husband and stellar detective.

I'd always operated on the right side of the law, just like my father had. Or so I thought. Yet if he was related to Antonio, perhaps he wasn't as saintly as my mother made him out to be. I wasn't entirely certain I wanted to know who he really was because I was happy with the polished version of my father.

Yet I knew Rhonda was right. It was better to know the truth about him, no matter how painful it may be. Besides, there was no getting around my bestie—one way or the other, she was determined to find out what was inside that envelope.

I picked up my purse and ran my hand over the package one more time, before handing it over to her.

"Will you do the honors?"

"Sure thing." Rhonda ripped it open without hesitation. "Would you look at that—there's a photo album and letter inside."

I took ahold of the photo album, noting the name printed on the front—Carmino Corozza. Seeing that combination set off a flurry of emotions racing through me. Since meeting Dottoressa Bianci, I'd had the sneaking suspicion that Antonio Corozza may be a relative. But seeing my father's own name printed before my enemy's hurt more than I had expected.

"Who is Carmino Corozza?" Rhonda asked.

I looked up at my bestie, already knowing that my answer was going to make her mouth circle up into an O. "He was my father."

As expected, Rhonda's shocked expression almost made me giggle. "But why is your last name De Luca?"

"I honestly don't know. I think my grandmother has some explaining to do later. Or perhaps the Dottoressa's letter will answer that question. I'll get to that in a minute."

I opened the book, slowly flipping through the pages filled with my father's childhood photos. His first dog, his first bike, his first car, his first girlfriend—Bianci had documented it all. It broke my heart to see him so young and vulnerable. The only photos I'd seen of my dad were of him playing sports with friends, chumming around with his police buddies, or sitting behind the wheel of a squad car.

Rhonda let me view the photos in peace, but once I closed the cover, she asked, "Can I take a look?"

"Sure. They're all new to me. I've never seen any photos of him from before he moved to America."

I wiped a tear from my eye, then opened the letter.

In a flowery handwriting that was challenging to read, Bianci explained that my father was Antonio's younger brother by fifteen years. Their father had been a high-ranking lieutenant in the local mafia, and Antonio had gladly followed in his footsteps, eventually rising to the top of the organization. My father's last name was Corozza, not De Luca. He'd changed it when he moved to America, choosing the most common Italian name he could think of in the hopes his brother would not easily find him. Yet Antonio did. After Carmino had been promoted to detective, Antonio reached out, asking him to pass along information. When Carmino refused, Antonio accused him of turning against the family, they fought, and Antonio lost control and murdered my father in a fit of rage.

Reading that did cause many tears to fall. Even though I'd never met him, it was deeply saddening to know that my father had been murdered for doing the right thing.

A wave of anger followed next, along with a blast of insight. For almost four years, I had been consumed with finding Antonio in order to exact some sort of revenge for my husband's death. Yet if Antonio could kill his own brother—my father—so heartlessly, then Reggie was right. Antonio probably wouldn't remember Carlos, let alone how he died. Which meant I would never know why my husband was murdered, or whether Antonio had pulled the trigger. And confronting that psychopath to learn nothing was not worth dying for.

"Carmen—are you alright? Your face is paling pretty fast. Is it bad news?"

I looked up at Rhonda, taking in her concerned expression. I had been so caught up in Bianci's words, I'd forgotten that she was still sitting next to me. "Not really, just depressing. Let me finish reading it, then I'll let you take a look."

I couldn't bring yet myself to tell her that Antonio Corozza—the mob boss she knew I had been searching for—was my uncle.

She laid a hand on my arm and squeezed, before flipping to the next page of my dad's photo album. Like a true friend, she trusted that I would open up to her, when I was ready to do so. I picked the letter back up, determined to get through the last two pages before breaking down completely.

The letter continued, "Carmino should have disappeared again, instead of confronting Antonio. But he thought he could make his brother understand why he wanted to break free from the family and build up a new life in America. But Antonio did not understand, not at all. Which is why Carmino is dead. He was my favorite nephew and sole heir. Now, everything goes to you."

That last line took my breath away. I flipped to the final page and took a closer look at the numbers and line items listed. It was an overview of the Dottoressa's substantial holdings, as well as the current value of her financial portfolio. Based on that amount, I was about to become a seriously wealthy woman. Not only did Bianci set me up with a healthy bank account, she also left me a palazzo in Venice and a winery in Tuscany, just outside of Florence. I hadn't expected anything from her, and certainly not all of this.

But what really got my attention was her last reference to another package her lawyer had sent to a number of law enforcement organizations, including Interpol and the Italian police, shortly after her death. She described it as a thick folder of information about Antonio's organization and their shady dealings. According to Bianci, it contained enough evidence to ensure that Antonio would finally be arrested and made to pay for his many crimes.

"Retribution is my gift to you. I should have done this years ago, after

Carmino, but I was afraid. I have no children of my own and nothing more to fear. Consider this part of your inheritance."

I stared off into the distance, silently contemplating the ramifications of the intel in Bianci's letter. Would it be enough to dismantle his organization? Would I ever have the chance to interrogate him, and perhaps discover the truth about my husband, after all? The idea that Antonio would pay for his crimes, or at least some of them, was an exceedingly pleasant one.

"Can I take a look at the letter, too?"

Rhonda's question broke my train of thought.

"Sure." I handed over everything except the last page, letting her read through it while I took in all that my great-aunt had left me.

When Rhonda got to the end, she waggled her eyebrows at me. "So what's the bottom line? She mentions leaving everything to you, but what is everything?"

"About twenty million euros, a palazzo in Venice, and a winery in Tuscany."

"Oh la la! You're one of us *nouveau riche* now!"

"My gosh, you're right." Technically, I was now as rich as many of those I targeted. That idea made my head spin.

I took a deep breath, letting this news sink in. As I did, I felt an incredible sense of joy as I realized the universe was providing me with new and exciting opportunities.

"Do you want to be a sleuth still?"

"I don't know." I squeezed Rhonda's hand as I looked over the last page of Bianci's letter one more time. Her inheritance changed everything.

"Ask me that again next week, after I've gotten a real tan. For right now, I think it's better to take it one day at a time."

Rhonda threw her arm over my shoulder. "That's the spirit, Carmen!"

THE END

Thanks for reading *A Killer Inheritance*!

Reviews really do help readers decide whether they want to take a chance on a new author. If you enjoyed this story, please consider posting a review on BookBub, on Goodreads, or with your favorite retailer.

I appreciate it! Jennifer S. Alderson

Acknowledgements

I am indebted to my editor, Sadye Scott-Hainchek of The Fussy Librarian, for her outstanding work and advice. The cover designer for this series and my Travel Can Be Murder Cozy Mysteries, Elizabeth Mackey, continues to amaze me with her gorgeous and fun designs.

Many thanks to my wonderful family for helping me create time to write, as well as for encouraging me to keep developing these new characters. I am so grateful for their love and support.

About the Author

Jennifer S. Alderson was born in San Francisco, grew up in Seattle, and currently lives in Amsterdam. After traveling extensively around Asia, Oceania, and Central America, she lived in Darwin, Australia, before settling in the Netherlands.

Jennifer's love of travel, art, and culture inspires her award-winning Zelda Richardson Mystery series, her Travel Can Be Murder Cozy Mysteries, and her Carmen De Luca Art Sleuth Mysteries. Her background in journalism, multimedia development, and art history enriches her novels.

When not writing, she can be found perusing a museum, biking around Amsterdam, or enjoying a coffee along the canal while planning her next research trip.

Visit Jennifer's website [https://jennifersalderson.com] to sign up for her newsletter. Subscribers receive updates on future releases, as well as *A Book To Die For*, a short cozy mystery, for free.

Books by Jennifer S. Alderson:

Carmen De Luca Art Sleuth Mysteries
Collecting Can Be Murder
A Statue To Die For
Forgeries and Fatalities
A Killer Inheritance

Travel Can Be Murder Cozy Mysteries
Death on the Danube: A New Year's Murder in Budapest

Death by Baguette: A Valentine's Day Murder in Paris
Death by Windmill: A Mother's Day Murder in Amsterdam
Death by Bagpipes: A Summer Murder in Edinburgh
Death by Fountain: A Christmas Murder in Rome
Death by Leprechaun: A Saint Patrick's Day Murder in Dublin
Death by Flamenco: An Easter Murder in Seville
Death by Gondola: A Springtime Murder in Venice
Death by Puffin: A Bachelorette Party Murder in Reykjavik
Death by Oxcart: An Independence Day Murder in Costa Rica

Zelda Richardson Art Mysteries
The Lover's Portrait: An Art Mystery
Rituals of the Dead: An Artifact Mystery
Marked for Revenge: An Art Heist Thriller
The Vermeer Deception: An Art Mystery

Standalone Travel Thriller
Down and Out in Kathmandu: A Backpacker Mystery

Death on the Danube: A New Year's Murder in Budapest

Book One of the Travel Can Be Murder Cozy Mystery series

Who knew a New Year's trip to Budapest could be so deadly? The tour must go on—even with a killer in their midst…

Recent divorcee Lana Hansen needs a break. Her luck has run sour for going on a decade, ever since she got fired from her favorite job as an investigative reporter. When her fresh start in Seattle doesn't work out as planned, Lana ends up unemployed and penniless on Christmas Eve.

Dotty Thompson, her landlord and the owner of Wanderlust Tours, is also in a tight spot after one of her tour guides ends up in the hospital, leaving her a guide short on Christmas Day.

When Dotty offers her a job leading the tour group through Budapest, Hungary, Lana jumps at the chance. It's the perfect way to ring in the new year and pay her rent!

What starts off as the adventure of a lifetime quickly turns into a nightmare when Carl, her fellow tour guide, is found floating in the Danube River. Was it murder or accidental death? Suspects abound when Lana discovers almost everyone on the tour had a bone to pick with Carl.

But Dotty insists the tour must go on, so Lana finds herself trapped with nine murder suspects. When another guest turns up dead, Lana has to figure out who the killer is before she too ends up floating in the Danube.

Excerpt from *Death on the Danube*

Chapter One: A Trip to Budapest

December 26—Seattle, Washington

"You want me to go where, Dotty? And do what?" Lana Hansen had trouble keeping the incredulity out of her voice. She was thrilled, as always, by her landlord's unwavering support and encouragement. But now Lana was beginning to wonder whether Dotty Thompson was becoming mentally unhinged.

"To escort a tour group in Budapest, Hungary. It'll be easy enough for a woman of your many talents."

Lana snorted with laughter. *Ha! What talents?* she thought. Her resume was indeed long: disgraced investigative journalist, injured magician's assistant, former kayaking guide, and now part-time yoga instructor—emphasis on "part-time."

"You'll get to celebrate New Year's while earning a paycheck and enjoying a free trip abroad, to boot. You've been moaning for months about wanting a fresh start. Well, this is as fresh as it gets!" Dotty exclaimed, causing her Christmas-bell earrings to jangle. She was wrapped up in a rainbow-colored bathrobe, a hairnet covering the curlers she set every morning. They were standing inside her living room, Lana still wearing her woolen navy jacket and rain boots. Behind Dotty's ample frame, Lana could see the many decorations and streamers she'd helped to hang up for the Christmas bash last night. Lana was certain that if Dotty's dogs hadn't woken her up, her landlord would have slept the day away.

"Working as one of your tour guides wasn't exactly what I had in mind, Dotty."

"I wouldn't ask you if I had any other choice." Dotty's tone switched from flippant to pleading. "Yesterday one of the guides and two guests crashed into each other while skibobbing outside of Prague, and all are hospitalized. Thank goodness none are in critical condition. But the rest of the group is leaving for Budapest in the morning, and Carl can't do it on his own. He's just not client-friendly enough to pull it off. And I need those five-star reviews,

Lana."

Dotty was not only a property manager, she was also the owner of several successful small businesses. Lana knew Wanderlust Tours was Dotty's favorite and that she would do anything to ensure its continued success. Lana also knew that the tour company was suffering from the increased competition from online booking sites and was having trouble building its audience and generating traffic to its social media accounts. But asking Lana to fill in as a guide seemed desperate, even for Dotty, and even if it was the day after Christmas. Lana shook her head slowly. "I don't know. I'm not qualified to—"

Dotty grabbed one of Lana's hands and squeezed. "Qualified, shmalified. I didn't have any tour guide credentials when I started this company fifteen years ago, and that hasn't made a bit of difference. You enjoy leading those kayaking tours, right? This is the same thing, but for a while longer."

The older lady glanced down at the plastic cards in her other hand, shaking her head. "Besides, you know I love you like a daughter, but I can't accept these gift cards in lieu of rent. If you do this for me, you don't have to pay me back for the past two months' rent. I am offering you the chance of a lifetime. What have you got to lose?"

If you are enjoying the book, why not pick up your copy now and keep reading? Available as paperback, large print edition, eBook, audiobook, and in Kindle Unlimited.

The Lover's Portrait: An Art Mystery

Book One in the Zelda Richardson Art Mystery Series

"*The Lover's Portrait* is a well-written mystery with engaging characters and a lot of heart. The perfect novel for those who love art and mysteries!" – Reader's Favorite, 5-star medal

"Well worth reading for what the main character discovers—not just about the portrait mentioned in the title, but also the sobering dangers of Amsterdam during World War II." – IndieReader

A portrait holds the key to recovering a cache of looted artwork, secreted away during World War II, in this captivating historical art thriller set in the 1940s and present-day Amsterdam.

When a Dutch art dealer hides the stock from his gallery—rather than turn it over to his Nazi blackmailer—he pays with his life, leaving a treasure trove of modern masterpieces buried somewhere in Amsterdam, presumably lost forever. That is, until American art history student Zelda Richardson sticks her nose in.

After studying for a year in the Netherlands, Zelda scores an internship at the prestigious Amsterdam Historical Museum, where she works on an exhibition of paintings and sculptures once stolen by the Nazis, lying unclaimed in Dutch museum depots almost seventy years later. When two women claim the same painting, the portrait of a young girl entitled *Irises*, Zelda is tasked with investigating the painting's history and soon finds evidence that one of the two women must be lying about her past. Before she can figure out which one it is and why, Zelda learns about the Dutch art dealer's concealed collection. And that *Irises* is the key to finding it all.

Her discoveries make her a target of someone willing to steal—and even kill—to find the missing paintings. As the list of suspects grows, Zelda realizes she has to track down the lost collection and unmask a killer if she wants to survive.

Excerpt from *The Lover's Portrait*
Chapter 1: Two More Crates

June 26, 1942

Just two more crates, then our work is finally done, Arjan reminded himself as he bent down to grasp the thick twine handles, his back muscles already yelping in protest. Drops of sweat were burning his eyes, blurring his vision. "You can do this," he said softly, heaving the heavy oak box upwards with an audible grunt.

Philip nodded once, then did the same. Together they lugged their loads across the moonlit room, down the metal stairs, and into the cool subterranean space below. After hoisting the last two crates onto a stack close to the ladder, Arjan smiled in satisfaction, slapping Philip on the back as he regarded their work. One hundred and fifty-two crates holding his most treasured objects, and those of so many of his friends, were finally safe. Relief briefly overcame the panic and dread he'd been feeling for longer than he could remember. Preparing the space and artwork had taken more time than he'd hoped it would, but they'd done it. Now he could leave Amsterdam knowing he'd stayed true to his word. Arjan glanced over at Philip, glad he'd trusted him. He stretched out a hand towards the older man. "They fit perfectly."

Philip answered with a hasty handshake and a tight smile before nodding towards the ladder. "Shall we?"

He is right, Arjan thought, *there is still so much to do*. They climbed back up into the small shed and closed the heavy metal lid, careful to cushion its fall. They didn't want to give the neighbors an excuse to call the Gestapo. Not when they were so close to being finished.

Philip picked up a shovel and scooped sand onto the floor, letting Arjan rake it out evenly before adding more. When the sand was an inch deep, they shifted the first layer of heavy cement tiles into place, careful to fit them snug up against each other.

As they heaved and pushed, Arjan allowed himself to think about the future for the first time in weeks. Hiding the artwork was only the first step; he still had a long way to go before he could stop looking over his shoulder. First, back to his place to collect their suitcases. Then, a short walk to Central Station where second-class train tickets to Venlo were waiting. Finally, a taxi ride to the Belgian border where his contact would provide him with falsified travel documents and a chauffeur-driven Mercedes-Benz. The five Rembrandt etchings in his suitcase would guarantee safe passage to Switzerland. From Geneva he should be able to make his way through the demilitarized zone to Lyon, then down to Marseilles. All he had to do was keep a few steps ahead of Oswald Drechsler.

Just thinking about the hawk-nosed Nazi made him work faster. So far he'd been able to clear out his house and storage spaces without Drechsler noticing. Their last load, the canvases stowed in his gallery, was the riskiest, but he'd had no choice. His friends trusted him—no, counted on him—to keep their treasures safe. He couldn't let them down now. Not after all he'd done wrong.

If you are enjoying what you are reading, why not pick up your copy now and keep reading? Available as eBook, audiobook, and paperback.

www.ingramcontent.com/pod-product-compliance
Lightning Source LLC
LaVergne TN
LVHW041712070526
838199LV00045B/1309